Bond of Love

Letters From Home Series

By
Maryann Jordan

Bond of Love (Letters From Home Series)
Copyright © 2017 Maryann Jordan

Cover Design by: Sommer Stein
Editor: Shannon Brandee Eversoll
ISBN: 978-0-9984832-3-8

Dedication

As a high school counselor, I worked with many students who joined the military after high school. A few of them I stayed close to and watched as they matured during their enlistment. I know letters from home meant so much to them and they were the idea behind these stories. For those, and all who have served, I dedicate this story to them.

Author Notes

When writing military romance, I desire to portray accurately the soldiers' jobs, duties, and situations, but know that in some areas I will fall short simply because I have never walked in their boots. I hope my readers will focus on the love story, while appreciating the service from our men and women in the military.

Chapter 1

(March – Ben)

I opened the door to the supply closet and there he was, humping the new nurse from behind...honest to God, I'm not making this shit up! They looked over at me and stopped what they were doing (I swear the look they gave me was as though they hoped I had no clue what was going on, but I assure you, I knew what they were doing!!!) and all I did was grab what I needed and then say, "Sorry, please continue" as I walked out and shut the door behind me! I swear, it's like working in a fucking zoo...literally!!!

JAMES HAD TO stop reading, the men around him were laughing so hard. He looked over at his squad, some hanging down from their bunks with their eyes on him, and said, "Honest to God, she's told me this stuff goes on all the time."

Between chuckles, I asked, "Hell, does anyone get taken care of at the hospital or is the staff just screwing each other?"

"Hey, I don't know about anyone else," James protested, "but my sister's a good nurse…and I know she doesn't screw around in supply closets!"

I threw my hands up in defense. "I didn't mean Alicia! But her letters are fuckin' hilarious!"

Another squad member ducked in through the door letting in a gust of cold, Afghanistan wind and hurried into the small room, amidst cursing the freezing blast. "What'd I miss? One of Alicia's letters?" Looking around, Roger saw the others still sniggering and pouted, "Oh, damn. You started without me."

Our tent was heated, for which I was grateful, but we still huddled in our coats as we lounged on the bunk beds. Our twelve-member squad shared the tent, three bunk beds on either side of a center aisle. We'd slept on cots in the field but, here on base, our bunks held real mattresses, considered a step-up in accommodations. We each had a footlocker as well as a tall locker next to our bunks to keep our personal items. The floors were wooden, scuffed, and worn planks but much better than the dirt.

I grinned at the men around me, their smiles easier now that they were back at the base rather than the middle of the god-forsaken, mountainous region of Afghanistan. I waved Roger on in, saying, "You can catch up, man. All you missed was the sex in the supply closet."

"Fuck!" Roger cursed, throwing himself down in a chair. "I missed the best part!"

The others laughed again, as James smoothed out the pieces of paper and continued to read.

Dr. Simmons, the surgeon whose head is so big I can't figure out how his scrawny neck holds it up, has asked me out again. I've turned him down at least four times and he just doesn't get it. I think when I say, "No, I am not interested" he hears, "I'd love to at another time!" What is it with guys that don't listen? (Okay, not you brother dear — you've always listened!)

I did actually go on a date with a man I met in the coffee shop. He was cute, struck up a conversation and is a pharmaceutical rep visiting at the hospital. So we go to dinner (yes, I met him at the restaurant and did not give him my address) and during the dinner his phone rings. He takes the call, while I'm sitting there, and has a conversation with his WIFE!!!

Sooooo, I walked out, leaving him sitting all alone. Anyway, I've decided that I will not waste my time on men who will never be Mr. Right. My long shifts in the ER leave me too tired to date now anyway!

You are always telling me how great your squad members are...why aren't they single and knocking down my door?? Just kidding!

I know you can't tell me much about what you're doing or where you are, but know I miss you terribly! Take care!

Love, your sis!

Alicia

I shook my head and said, "Man, those guys your sister goes out with are fuckin' idiots! I can't imagine what's going through their minds." I'd seen pictures of his sister and knew she was a looker.

"I know. Jesus, she's smart, has a good job, and is gorgeous," James replied. He rubbed his hand over his military-short dark hair.

"Which one of you is older?" Roger asked.

"You didn't know?" I asked, glancing over my shoulder. "Alicia is his twin."

"Twin? Do you guys look alike?"

James and I laughed as he replied, "No, dumb-ass. Only identical twins look alike. You can't have a guy and a girl be identical twins."

Roger blushed, but his scrunched face appeared confused as though he had never thought of that explanation before.

I turned back to James and added, "But I have to admit, you two do look a lot alike...except she's a helluva lot prettier!"

Grinning, James leaned back, stretching his arms

over his head and said, "Never had any women complaining about my looks so far!"

Shaking my head, I chuckled as I lay back down on my cot, my mind soon turning over to the duties of tomorrow.

★

"I'M DONE WITH mine. You need help?" I asked James as I walked over to the wrecked Humvee he was busy taking apart. Pieces of metal were piled up all around him on the ground, along with engine parts.

James nodded as he cursed. "The wind keeps the fuckin' Moon Dust swirled up so I can hardly see what I'm doing."

One of the difficulties we dealt with was the layer of dust on the ground that was quickly swirled up when the wind blew—and the wind always blew. It not only made daily life unpleasant but for those of us who worked in areas that needed to stay clean, it presented an ongoing problem.

Nodding my acknowledgment, I joined in to help him, as did a few other mechanics, and together we made quick work of dismantling the unusable vehicle. "I heard this one came in today and figured you'd have to take it apart," I commented to James.

"We've got wrecker duty this weekend, but maybe

it'll be a quiet one," James said, as he salvaged a door.

This Humvee had hit an IED and part of our job as combat mechanics was to go out into the field when a vehicle was destroyed and recover it. Nothing was to be left for the Afghans or Taliban to reclaim and possibly use.

Tossing pieces of metal from the roof to the ground, I jumped down and began stacking what I could. Another mechanic checked the tires, salvaging two of them and moving them to the side. By the end of our shift, most of the Humvee was dismantled and the parts were taken to where they would be used to rebuild damaged vehicles that could get back on the road.

After our shift, I hit the showers, washing off the sweat, dirt, and grime that came from working outside and on vehicles. I'd loved working on cars for as long as I could remember and being a combat mechanic had been the perfect job for me, but dismantling wasn't as satisfying as repairing. Stepping out of the shower, toweling off, I dressed in a clean Army Combat Uniform in the locker room with the others from our squad on the same shift. The Afghan nationals that worked in the laundry always did a good job on our ACUs and it felt good to put on clean clothes.

"God, I'm hungry," I said as we walked outside, heading to the Dining Facility. "Wonder what culinary delights the DFAC has for us tonight?"

"I'd eat anything," Roger replied, "but I sure hope

they've got some good desserts left."

"I'll catch up to you guys. If they're running out of cake, save me some," James called out, turning toward another tent on the right of the main lane.

"You gonna hit the mail tent before eating?" I asked.

"Yeah," James nodded. "You coming?"

"Hell, you know no one ever writes to me! That's why I live vicariously through you!" With a wave, I headed into the large DFAC tent, the tantalizing smells drawing my interest.

★

A FEW WEEKS later, I lay back on my bunk, too tired to even read a book. After work, the squad had joined a pick-up basketball game, during which I realized my body wasn't as young as it used to be. A lot of the younger recruits were only eighteen or nineteen years old since many soldiers only stayed for one tour. There were less of us who were pushing ten years in and that was more noticeable when going head to head in a ruthless basketball game. Hearing a noise at the front of the tent, I glanced over.

James walked in, a smile on his face as he carried a box in his hands. "Look what I've got!"

Recognizing a care package from Alicia, I found the energy to sit up knowing something good would be inside. I hoped it would be some of her tasty cookies, but knew first he'd read her letter. And that was okay…her letters always put us in a good mood.

Hey James,

I've got some family gossip this time! You know how we always thought Aunt Cora was so high and mighty all the time, and you used to say that she probably had some kind of secret life 'cause no one could be so sanctimonious? Well, guess who's been having an affair for the past year? Yep, she's been banging her neighbor! And the story gets weirder…Uncle Charles found out about it and he and the neighbor's wife started an affair also! They began just out of spite with their spouses' affair, but then they fell in love. So Uncle Charles and Aunt Cora are getting a divorce. He's moved in with his neighbor and they are planning on getting married. But, the real crazy part is that Cora and her lover, split up! How funny is that??

Work has been the same. I like the ER, but sometimes I wonder how long I can keep this up — the pace is insane. It was easier when I was first out of nursing school, but I'm starting to feel the fatigue from these hours. I know when you were home last, we talked about the different places I could work, but I just can't figure out what I want. I wish you were here — it's always so much easier when we can talk things through. I won't make any changes now, but when you come home next, we'll talk more about my choices.

I have no fun sex-in-the-closet stories in this letter...everyone must either be tired or hiding!

My car's been making the strangest noises lately, but seems to be running okay. I know, I know — I should take it in. There's just no time! Now, if you were here...(hint!) I got so used to you always keeping an eye on it for me.

Please take care and come home soon! Mom and dad will send another care package next week! These cookies are from me!

Love you,
Alicia

I looked over at James as he finished reading her letter out loud, recognizing the wistful expression that he always got when Alicia wrote to him. I figured as twins, they must share an unusual bond. Hell, with my fucked up background, I had no idea what a familial bond was like, but I could appreciate it in my friend...*and be envious.*

Sitting up on my bed, I peeked into the box on the floor between us. "Cookies! Hell, yeah!" Reaching inside, I grabbed one of the plastic baggies packed carefully and tore one open. "Nothing quite like Alicia's chocolate chip cookies," I groaned, my mouth full of chocolatey goodness.

"Leave me some," James protested, grabbing another baggie. Popping one into his mouth, he smiled as he chewed. "God, I love my sister! This is just what I needed."

"You're lucky, man."

"I know," he agreed. "It's always been like this. Like we knew each other's thoughts before we spoke them." He shrugged, adding, "We just always got each other, you know? That brother-sister bond thing that most siblings have, we got in spades."

Never having had siblings, I wondered what that must be like. *At least I get to enjoy the benefits*, I thought as I chewed another cookie.

There was only one more bag left and James shared it with the other members of our squad that were not on shift that night. As Roger walked in, he said, "I just heard the wrecker's going out tomorrow. One of the big M35 cargo trucks hit an IED and blew the side off."

We all froze as we stared at Roger. Our first thought was if any soldiers had been injured. Roger's typically joking smile was absent.

"Fuck," James and I said in unison, as I knew we would be the ones to go out for the reclaiming duty tomorrow.

The taste of Alicia's cookie was no longer as sweet in my mouth, thinking about the upcoming job, and the constant threat that we would be driving over the same war-torn terrain.

Chapter 2

(April – Alicia)

M Y FEET WERE dragging as I walked out to the
hospital's employee parking lot. A twelve-hour
shift as an ER nurse had drained me of all my energy. It
was moments like this I wished I lived closer to the
hospital, but thirty minutes later when I turned onto my
neighborhood street, I smiled. It had been a risk, moving
from my close-to-the-hospital apartment I shared with
two other nurses to buying a small, starter home in an
older neighborhood. Turning off the engine, I watched
as the setting sun illuminated the front of my house and
I knew the risk had paid off...in spades.

Walking to my front door, I reached into my mailbox and pulled out a handful of envelopes. I loved how
this neighborhood had the mailboxes attached to the
house so that I could grab my mail easily and not have to
run to the street. *Funny, how the little things in life make
me happy!*

Quickly shuffling through the mail as I entered the

house, I found the one that always brought a smile to my lips. A letter from James. *Twins and friends since birth*, mom always said.

Tiger, my large striped cat, immediately circled my legs to be fed. Knowing she wouldn't leave me alone until I acknowledged—and took care of—her stomach, I hustled into the kitchen. Pouring some food into her dish, I grinned as she began to crunch her dinner.

Kicking off my colorful, Dansko professional clogs, I wiggled my toes in the thick rug and plopped down on the sofa. Ripping open the envelope, I leaned back as Tiger jumped into my lap. With one hand petting her soft fur, the other held the pieces of paper, filled with lines of James' crooked handwriting.

Hey Alicia,

I keep promising myself I will stop writing these ridiculous snail mail letters and just type an email...but then you would moan and groan like you always do, telling me that letter writing is a dying art. Okay – fine, but don't complain if you can't read my handwriting!

Things are the same here. There is always a shit-ton of vehicles to maintain and repair. A few weeks ago, I was in the field with Ben and there was a huge truck that had hit an explosion and was on its side. We had to take the wrecker out to get it righted and then haul it back to base. I wasn't sure if it could be rebuilt, but yours truly can work magic! We just got that monster truck back into business!

Speaking of Ben, I swear, he's so much better than any of those jerks you've been dating. I wish you could meet him sometime. When we get back home, I'll introduce you to him. In the meantime, watch out for that prick of a doctor – if he tries anything, knee him in the nuts. That's something all men will understand as a "no"!

Okay, this is short, but I swear my hand is already cramping. Next time, sis, you get an email! The guys all say thanks for the care package. Your cookies are the best and that opinion is shared by all the men in my squad. Tell mom and dad hi for me.

Love from your older brother (okay, by only 1 minute, but I figure it counts!),

James

Grinning, I slid further down on the sofa with my

head leaned back and propped my socked feet up on the coffee table, letting Tiger massage my tummy with her paws. My gaze drifted to the mantle over the fireplace that I had never used, admittedly too afraid of any creatures that may have taken up residence there. The polished, dark walnut mantle held my treasures...family pictures depicting me and James from infancy to the last time he was home on leave, almost a year ago. Sighing, I quickly calculated how much more time until I could see him again. Nine months. *We got this, bro!*

★

A RARE SUNDAY off from work, and I decided to drop by to see mom and dad. My stomach had felt queasy all day and hoped I wasn't getting sick. My parents lived almost an hour away, but I knew dad would be piled up in his recliner watching baseball and mom would love having some company.

As soon as I walked into their house, the scent of mom's ambrosia cookies filled the air. "Oh, my God, mom!" I squealed, calling out a hasty hello to my dad in the living room as I ran into the kitchen. Grabbing mom around the waist, I hugged her tightly. "I love these and so will James! I told him you would send him a care package soon!" Her ambrosia cookies were chock full of raisins, chopped dates, oatmeal, and coconut. Thick and chewy, just the way James and I liked them.

Mom twisted, throwing her arms around me as well, her eyes twinkling. "Hey, baby girl," she said, her smile as wide as mine. Letting me go, she held me at arm's length as she scanned me from head to toe and added, "You need to eat more, Alicia. I swear, that hospital job has you run off your feet." She peered deeply into my eyes and cocked her head to the side. "Something seems off. What's wrong?"

"I've felt a little queer ever since I got up this morning," I admitted. "And with my job schedule, I've lost a couple of pounds, but I'll bet this will help," I said, grabbing one of her cookies off the cooling rack.

She attempted to smack me with a rolled up dish towel but had never perfected the act the way James could. When we were kids I'd have to run away when he was playing with a towel and trying to snap me.

An hour later, as all the cookies had been baked and were now cooling, mom and I joined dad in the living room with tea and snacks. The lazy Sunday with my parents in the house I grew up in was the perfect way to spend a day off. Relaxing, fun, peaceful…except for my nervous stomach.

One baseball game had finished and another one just came on when dad looked out the front window behind me, his face morphing from curiosity to a wide-eyed stare.

"Dad?" I questioned before turning around to see what had captured his attention. A dark vehicle had pulled into the driveway and two men in Army dress uniforms alighted.

Mom had walked over from her chair to look through the window and before dad could get out of his recliner, mom cried, "Oh, Lord, no!" and ran to the door as though if she got to the officers before they could make it to her porch, they would have no power over her. She threw her hands on the door, pressing them flat against it, chanting, "No, no, no, no," until dad came up behind her and placed his hands over hers. I stood, rooted to the floor, my stomach twisting as my heart pounded, watching the trauma unfold before me.

"Arlene, honey, let me open the door," and dad gently pulled her back against his chest as he reached around and turned the doorknob just as the two officers stepped up onto the porch.

Both men looked at my parents with sympathy and I felt the air leave the room with their words. "Sir, ma'am, are you Arlene and George Newton, parents of Specialist James Newton of the U.S. Army?"

Mom's head shook back and forth—not in answer to their question but with the same denial I felt. Dad nodded, his voice shaky as he replied, "Yes. Yes, we are. Please come in."

He pulled mom back further into the room, giving the officers a chance to step inside the house as well. I could not take my eyes off them, even as I gasped for air.

I wanted to block them out, make them leave, scream that they were in the wrong place with the wrong people.

But my wishes were not headed as the older of the two looked straight into my parents' eyes and said, "We are sorry to inform you that your son was killed..."

I never heard the rest of the words, the explanations, the special instructions...nothing. My dad helped my mom to the sofa before he turned to me, his hand outstretched. Shaking my head, I rushed out of the room, my queasy stomach rebelling as I threw myself onto the floor by the toilet, throwing up what I had eaten. A few minutes later, I stumbled back into the living room, kneeling at dad's feet, my head on his knees as my mom collapsed onto my dad's chest.

Dad held it together enough to talk to the officers, with one hand on me and the other around mom's shoulders.

James...my brother...my twin...the one person in the world I had an unbreakable bond with was now gone.

★

THE FLAG-DRAPED CASKET stood in stark relief against the bright blue sky with only a few white clouds floating by. I tried to listen to the words of the Army Chaplain but all I could think about was how James was never going to come racing into the house again...or toss a dinner roll across the table at me when mom wasn't watching...or threaten some guy who wanted to date me. I wanted to cry, but it seemed the tears had all dried up. The honor guard folded the flag and handed it formally to mom and the tears finally slid down my face once more.

Mom sat between dad and me, leaning heavily on him with his arm around her. His hand would reach out and stroke my shoulder occasionally.

Some of James' high school friends that were still in the area came as well as some Army friends who were still stateside. Before I was ready to say goodbye, it was time. Standing, I waited as mom and dad approached the casket, laid their hands on it and bowed their heads. As dad helped mom back to the car, I followed their example. Laying a rose on top of the gleaming wood, I leaned over and whispered, "I'll always love you, big brother."

★

COMING OFF AN overnight shift in the ER two weeks later, I dragged to my car, wondering how I was going to keep going. I had barely slept since James' funeral, but still worked my twelve-hour shifts. Driving home on auto-pilot, I was glad to pull into my driveway safely considering I had no recollection of the trip home. Even though it was almost eight in the morning, I realized I had not gotten my mail yesterday, when I saw a few envelopes peeking out the top of my mailbox. Grabbing them, I made my way inside tossing the mail onto the kitchen table. Staggering into the kitchen, I poured a large glass of milk and toasted a bagel.

Tiger was making her usual figure-eights between my legs and I bent to rub her head. Her purring turned into meows and I knew it was her signal that she was hungry. Pouring some food into her dish, I grabbed my food from the counter. Sitting down a few minutes later, I nibbled my light breakfast and looked at the bills.

I gasped at the sight of a letter, my address written in squiggly handwriting. Heart pounding, I picked it up, my hand shaking so much I could barely focus on the return address. It was as though my mind expected it to say SPC James Newton, but as I stared, I finally realized it was from SPC Benjamin Fowler.

I lay the envelope down on the table, unwilling to open it now, the pain too fresh to share it with someone from the Army wanting to express condolences. Sucking in a shuddering breath, I placed my dishes in the sink and took a quick shower before closing my room-darkening curtains and falling into bed.

My sleep, like every day, was fitful, filled with dark dreams and painful memories. Waking after a few hours, I laid in bed staring at the ceiling, wondering when I would find the energy to get up. The room was cloaked in darkness even though it was the middle of the day.

The weight on my chest felt heavy but I welcomed it. Grief had become my blanket—while it weighed me down it was a constant reminder of my loss.

Rolling to my side, I heaved a sigh as I looked at the clock. Knowing I had not slept enough, I also knew no more rest was coming. Letting out a deep breath, I sat up with my knees bent and my head in my hands. The ever-present ache did not leave but then, I hadn't expected it to go away. An errant tear escaped and I swiped at it randomly.

Climbing out of bed, I wandered into the kitchen and fixed half of a peanut butter and banana sandwich, which was as much as I felt like eating. Taking my saucer into the living room I saw the envelope still laying on the table where I left it. I stood, my body taut, for a moment as I stared at the handwriting on the letter—not James' and yet so similar. Knowing it would not get any easier, I had to admit that after resting I felt better equipped to cope with whatever the correspondence had to say, so I flopped into a chair and tore it open.

Dear Ms. Alicia Newton,

I know you don't know me, but I was a good friend of your brother, James. I want to say how sorry I am for your loss and to let you know that he is sorely missed here as well. He was a good soldier, a good friend, and a good man.

I closed my eyes as I leaned back, irritation flowing over me. I know everyone who expressed their condolences meant well and I'm glad everyone liked James, but my heart ached so deeply, I wasn't sure if I could stand one more person telling me what I already knew.

I walked over to the refrigerator and poured a glass of water, drinking deeply. Dropping my chin to my chest as I leaned my hands on the counter, I sighed heavily. Licking my lips, I raised my head, staring out of the window across the room. The sun was indeed shining, the blue sky of spring sending its warmth into the room. Fortified, I walked over to the table and picked up the letter on my way to the sofa where I laid back against the cushions to continue reading.

> But I know that you are very aware of your brother's good points. What you might not have known is what he shared with his squad members about his sister. He read your letters to us and we loved each and every one of them. He regaled us with tales of your work, which by the way, he was so proud of. He had us laughing with tales of your dates, and I have to let you know he trusted your judgment, even if he pretended to want to be there to threaten those guys to treat you right.

Gasping, I sat up, my mouth hanging open. *James read my letters out loud? How embarrassing!* I felt my face flaming and if James had still been alive, I would have perfected the art of towel snapping just to make sure I nailed him good!

Taking a deep breath, I leaned back and continued to read.

> He also shared your care packages with us, for which we were all grateful. You make the best chocolate chip cookies of anyone I know.
>
> The most important thing I want to say is this...James loved you so much. I don't have any family so I used to joke that I lived vicariously through his family. So in a way, it's a double loss for me. Anyway, I thought it was important for you to know that he thought the world of you and I wish you all the peace you need during this time. I miss him too.
>
> Yours truly,
> SPC Benjamin Fowler

The tears came once more as I fell back on the sofa, the letter laying across my chest.

Chapter 3

(May – Ben)

I WALKED THROUGH the large tent covering the line of trucks we were working on that day, making my way to the transmission repair that was my assignment. Roger rolled out from underneath the truck he was working on and peered up at me.

"You doin' okay, man?"

Nodding, I curtly said, "Yeah, no worries." But I knew they were all worried—hell, I was worried about myself. Not about cracking up or going postal, but it was as though all the joy had been sucked out of me when James was killed. Sarge even had me go see the psych doc, who just agreed with my assessment—good soldiers die in war, and people left behind grieve them. *Hell, it's not rocket science…just a fact of life.*

Kneeling to the ground where truck guts were spilled out everywhere, I got to work. This world was familiar—at least with the machinery, I knew what to do to make it run and function correctly, even if I didn't have a clue for myself. I could take the pieces apart and put them back together again. I could find replacement parts and make them work when the original ones were no longer viable. But me? Hell, grief was tearing me apart inside. Closing my eyes for a moment, I thought of James' family—how are they coping? If my grief for a friend was killing me, then how did they manage the grief of a beloved son and brother?

I had sent James' sister a letter to let her know I was thinking about her but knew I had no clue what she was going through. I knew the other men in our squad suffered as well, but James and I had been friends since boot camp. Grimacing, I forced the thoughts from my mind, instead focusing on the engine parts in front of me.

Hours later, in the shower, I heard one of the guys call out. "Fowler...you got mail to pick up." *Mail? Me?* Sighing, I thought about what might be there...my bills were paid automatically and I had no one to write to me. *Probably junk.*

Heading to the DFAC with Roger, we walked down the main lane lined with look-alike tents. All tan and all bland. The sameness added to my desolate, morose feeling.

Roger glanced toward me. "You gettin' your mail before eating? They might not be open afterward."

"Probably just trash mail, but you're right. No sense

in them having it clutter their space. Save me a seat and I'll be right over." Gaining his nod, I turned toward the tent serving as the post office.

Stopping inside I waited in line, trying not to be envious of the lucky fuckers who were walking out with padded envelopes, packages of all sizes, or letters. Scrubbing my hand over my face as I got to the front of the line and gave my name, the soldier turned and lifted a box from a shelf behind him and set it down on the counter. I looked up at him but his eyes were on the person behind me in line.

He looked back at me, irritated that I was holding up the line and barked, "You gonna take your box or not?"

"This is for me?" I asked, unable to keep the shock out of my voice.

He tapped his finger on the address label and said, "If you're Specialist Benjamin Fowler, then yeah, this is for you. Now take it and move on outta the queue! Others are waiting."

Stunned, I picked up the box, staring at it as I walked back out into the stifling hot, evening air. Turning the box around in my hands, I looked at the return address. My heart skipped a beat before my hands broke out into a sweat. Alicia Newton. *James' sister? James' sister sent me a package!*

The others from my squad had gone to get their meal, but I hurried back to our tent, wanting to open it in private. Entering, I breathed a sigh of relief that the tent was empty. Sitting on my bed, I ripped open the box and pulled out the packing material. Inside were three plastic baggies of chocolate chip cookies. *Jackpot!*

Tucked to the side of the cookies was an envelope and I carefully pulled it out. It seemed strange to see my name written in the familiar handwriting that had always been to James. Sucking in a deep breath, I let it out slowly as I pulled out the sheets of paper.

Dear SPC Benjamin Fowler,

I want to thank you for your beautiful letter. So many people at work give me their condolences, which is nice, but since they didn't know him, I find myself longing to talk to someone who did. My parents are struggling, especially mom, and I don't want to add to her burden.

It's still hard for me to realize he won't be coming through my door at the end of the tour. I lay in bed and think of him and wish—well, I suppose that does no good. Sorry, I didn't mean for the letter to be depressing.

I admit, when I first read your letter and discovered that James had been sharing my letters to you all, I was mortified! I might have even cussed a little. But then I realized that by sharing my letters with you all, it meant you were trusted by him. And if my dating misadventures gave you all some pleasure, then I suppose it was worth it!

I also wanted to send some cookies to you. At first I thought I would be too sad to make chocolate chips cookies ever again, but then I knew that James would want me to take care of his buddies.

I know this might sound strange but if you ever get a chance to write to me again, I'd love it. I find that I really want to hear stories about James...the James you knew. I have all my memories and I play them over and over in my head when I lay in bed and can't sleep, but I'd love to know more about the James that was your friend. If it's an imposition, please don't feel obligated!

Anyway, I can tell you that he always spoke highly of you and when I read that you didn't have a family to write to you, I decided to send my cookies to you.

Please stay safe and you may tell James' other buddies hello from me and share the cookies if you want. Thank you again.

Yours truly,
Alicia

I read the letter three times, each time feeling a warm place deep inside that I hadn't felt since James died. I decided to share the cookies with the squad, but the letter was all mine and I had no desire to share Alicia with the others. After tucking it safely into my footlocker, I jogged toward the DFAC. I knew it was selfish to keep her all to myself since James so easily talked about her, but all I felt was a possessive yearning to bond with someone struggling with the same grief that held me captive.

★

THE CALL CAME in for wrecker duty and I was up. Jacob Balston, one of the other mechanics, and I set out. Leaving base in a large, armored five-ton wrecker, we slowly made our way along the directed road. The M1089 was designed to recover damaged, immobilized, swamped, stuck, or overturned vehicles and could also tow them back to the maintenance area. Driving such a powerful vehicle could be a heady experience except for the overriding fear of what the enemy could do in their efforts to keep us from our destination. Focusing on the road, I occasionally wiped my palms on my pants as we bounced along the rutted tracks.

The Afghanistan sun was already beating down and the inside truck cab became a broiler with our full uniforms, boots, weapons, helmets, and armor-proof vests. We followed another convoy that was moving in the same direction. The road dust kicked up and only the lead vehicle was somewhat immune to the lack of visibility, as well as breathing in the ever present Moon Dust. Wiping my face, I cursed.

"This place is fuckin' miserable already and it's only

May," Jacob commented.

Nodding, I concentrated on driving directly behind the vehicle in front of me hoping not to become a casualty while sweat dripped down my face.

"You thinkin' of James?" he asked, turning to look at me as I cursed once more at the pothole we hit.

"Yeah, it's hard not to. He was out on something just like this when he ran over the IED. 'Course he was not in a convoy, so I guess we're lucky."

"I noticed you're staying right behind the truck in front of us."

"Fuck yeah!" I cursed again.

Coming to the fork in the road where we would leave the convoy, we drove a few more clicks toward the mountainous region before coming to the overturned Humvee. Analyzing the turn-around space and the angle of the downed vehicle, I decided on a course of action. "Doesn't look too bad," I said, glad that the job shouldn't take more than a couple of hours.

We climbed out of the wrecker and walked over to assess the damage. "Looks like the back of the Humvee took the hit," Jacob said as he made his way around.

"Engine looks okay," I surmised before we discussed the best way to get it upright. Going back, I climbed into the cab and maneuvered the wrecker in place. I lowered the stabilizer jacks on each side for recovery and craning operations.

The armored cab of our wrecker provided me protection against small arms fire, artillery shell splinters, and mine blasts, but Jacob had no such protection outside...*just like James*. We efficiently attached the wench's twin lines to the upper side and quickly re-entered the wrecker. It did not take long to right the Humvee. Grateful all lifting operations could be controlled from inside our vehicle, we worked efficiently together. Hooking up to tow took a bit longer than I would have liked, and I observed Jacob stepping carefully when moving away from the vehicle.

Loaded and ready to head back, I carefully turned the wrecker around, attempting to stay on the road as much as possible. *Fuck this fear!* Having been on wrecker detail before, I was accustomed to seeing vehicles blown up by IEDs, but it was a job...not personal. Now all I could think of was James and how his life ended. I heard Jacob sigh and I knew he was thinking the same thing. Driving back to base, thoughts of James continued to filter through my mind. And thinking of James made me think of Alicia.

As soon as we were close enough to have the base in sight, I let out a long breath as Jacob joked about us being just in time for supper. Pulling into the base's motor pool, we unhooked the Humvee, leaving it for salvaging another day.

"I'm hitting the showers before dinner," I called out

to Jacob.

Waving, he grinned and said, "I'm starving. I'm going to DFAC first and hopefully they'll still have some good desserts left."

Smiling, I agreed but my thoughts ran to wishing I had more of Alicia's chocolate chip cookies...and another letter.

★

STEPPING INTO THE tent a few nights later, I found some of the squad playing poker. As soon as their eyes landed on me, the competitive game was abandoned. I was carrying another package from the mailroom. The top was open and the grin on my face gave evidence as to what lay inside.

"Hell, yeah!" Roger shouted, first out of his chair. Rushing over, he looked at me with basset-hound eyes, begging, "Please tell me those are from James' sister."

The others soon surrounded me, their greedy hands out as we divided up the goodies. His mouth full of cookie, Jacob asked, "Why's she sending you stuff?" Swallowing, he added quickly, "Not that I'm complaining!"

Shrugging, I said, "I guess she just wants to keep feeding her brother's friends." Unwilling to add that she had included another letter to me, I let them simply appreciate the treats.

As they finished eating and went back to their game, I slipped outside to re-read her letter. I had just written her one in return but had not mailed it yet, wondering what I could offer. My heart ached reading her words again.

Dear Benjamin,

I'm afraid you will think of me as a stalker if I keep sending cookies, but baking James' favorites makes me feel better and I certainly don't need to eat them all. So, if I bake to feel less sad, then I'll send them to you to enjoy.

I dreamed of James last night, only it wasn't the usual dream of when we were kids. He was in his uniform and driving a truck. I have no idea why I saw him that way because in real life, I never saw him at his work with the Army. I still think of him first thing when I wake up and he is the last thing I think of when I go to sleep at night. I suppose that is why he is in my dreams. Does it sound weird to say that I don't mind these dreams? It's like I want any part of him...even if it is just in my imagination.

I promised myself I would keep this short, so I'll say goodbye. Enjoy the cookies.

Yours truly,
Alicia

Heaving a sigh, I thought of Alicia's sadness and wished I could make her happier. I knew then, I would mail the letter the next morning. If all I had to offer were words about her brother to give her comfort, then that was what I'd do. God knows, her letters were giving me peace.

Chapter 4

(June – Alicia)

*H*E MUST THINK *I'm desperate...or a stalker...or a complete bimbo!* Thoughts about Benjamin Fowler filled my mind as I wandered up and down the aisle of the grocery store. I'd been invited to a dinner party by Roberta, one of the nurses on my shift, and I'd promised to bring something, but nothing on the shelves was calling to me. I didn't feel like cooking, so I wandered to the bakery counter. Standing there staring at cookies, pies, and cakes only made me think of James. *Nope...not what I want.*

Finally, abandoning all pretenses of coming up with something original, I headed over to the deli section and bought a cheese ball. Placing it into my basket I tried to ignore how boring it was. *I need crackers to go with this.* Walking back through the whole store, I found crackers on the cookie aisle. Passing the chocolate chip cookies had me thinking about James again and wishing his friend had written.

Sighing, I pushed my almost empty cart down the frozen food aisle. Ice cream…the perfect I'm-in-a-bad-sad-terrible-mood food. Tossing the butter pecan and chocolate mint ice cream into the cart with the cheese ball and crackers, I made my way to the checkout counter.

Paying for my meager purchases, I drove home trying to decide what to wear. Grabbing the mail on my way inside, I made sure to put the cheese into the refrigerator and the ice cream into the freezer before turning back to the mail. Seeing the handwriting on the first envelope, I tossed the rest of the mail down as I mentally fist pumped.

Ripping the letter open once I settled onto the sofa and leaned back, I began to read.

Dear Alicia,

Thank you for the cookies! It was such a surprise to get the package - I was sure the mail worker had made a mistake. I understand your desire to know more about James and I am honored you chose me to fill you in. I've never done anything like this, so I'll try to do justice to your request.

James was a smart mechanic. We met in boot camp and bonded when we discovered we were both going for the same MOS. I'd worked on cars before the Army and figured I knew everything but it didn't take long to find out I had a lot to learn. Sometimes I'd get frustrated and it was James that would laugh and make me realize that there was no shame in needing to learn something new.

We ended up in the same squad and became really good friends. He could take apart an engine faster than anyone I knew and would offer to help the rest of us if we needed it. That was another thing about James, but you probably already knew this - he was always willing to help others. Truly selfless and a really good friend.

One thing he hated to do was dismantle a vehicle. That's kind of different, because some of the mechanics like doing that, but not James. I think maybe it was because he just hated to see any vehicle end up un-fixable. He was that way with people as well. If someone was down, he'd manage to joke them into laughing again.

I didn't mean to make you feel weird when I told you that he would read your letters. But James knew that your letters were a bit of home that we all missed. Like I said, for me, it was a chance to enjoy hearing about his family since I don't have any. He worried about you. He was so proud of you being a nurse, but he worried all the time. He thought you worked too hard and that your shifts in the ER were too long. I'd remind him that we worked long shifts too, but he'd throw his hand out dismissively. He always had your back!

He worried about who you dated also. He always said it would take someone special to deserve you. I'd have to say he was right. Anyway, I hope some of this helps you as you are dealing with the loss. I miss him, but am really glad we were able to connect through our good memories. Please take care of yourself. I guess with him gone, I feel responsible for worrying about you now.

Again, thanks for the care package!

Ben

As I finished the letter, the muscles in my face felt odd, and then I realized I was smiling. *When was the last time I smiled? Really smiled?* I knew the answer and it was before James was killed. I re-read the letter again, not wanting to miss any words. I noticed he addressed me as

Alicia and signed the missive as Ben. I liked that—less formal, more like friends.

I lay on the sofa, thoughts of James in the Army now floating through my mind based on Ben's words, and the pain seemed less sharp. Tiger jumped up on my lap and with a few circles curled up, her purrs matching my mood. I lost track of time until my phone beeped an incoming message and I jumped up to see one of the other nurses asking what I was bringing to the party.

Rushing through the house, I showered quickly and threw on a sundress with a matching Bolero jacket. With makeup hastily applied while blowing my hair dry, I was ready in record time. Grabbing the cheese and crackers, I headed back out.

Two hours later, I was ready to go back home. Dr. Ted Simmons managed to snag the seat next to me and on the other side was one of the new doctors. Both single, both interested, both obnoxious. While I sat in a verbal-bragging-tug-of-war between them, one of my nursing friends kept laughing as I rolled my eyes numerous times. As soon as the dessert was served, I jumped up offering to help with the cleanup. An escape to the bathroom provided another reprieve, until I was once more cornered by Dr. Simmons, who appeared unable to discern the difference between polite conversation and interest.

Just as I was attempting to move away, he said, "I

never got a chance to say I was really sorry to hear about your brother's death. I guess with him in the military, you were prepared for it to happen."

Turning slowly, I stared dumbfounded at him. "What?" I asked on a breath.

"You know? If you're going to join the military, you pretty much know you've got a good chance of getting killed, so I just figured you were prepared as well."

Stunned, I felt the white hot blast of anger hit me as my chest heaved in indignation. "No," I choked, "While I was always proud of his service, I did not expect him to die and to imply otherwise is just rude and presumptuous!" Turning on my heels, I stalked away, attempting to get as far away from him as possible while I blinked back tears.

Not wanting to be the first to leave, I was grateful that another couple was making their farewells to the host. I jumped at the chance to say goodbye as well. Once in my car driving home, I breathed easier. *Why is it so hard to meet a good man?*

The thought of Ben ran through my mind...*a good man.* He doesn't know me and yet has taken time to reach out to me, for no other purpose than to make me feel better. I suddenly wanted to know what he looked like—I wanted a face to go with the friend he was becoming. Remembering James' footlocker had been delivered to mom and dad, I determined to visit tomorrow.

With that thought, I put the disastrous dinner party out of my mind and smiled once more, for the second time that day.

★

"MOM? DAD?" I called out, entering their front door.

"In the back, Alicia!" mom yelled from the kitchen.

I walked in and saw her putting away groceries. She turned and smiled, offering a tight hug. I heard the lawn mower and glanced through the window, seeing dad walking along, pushing the mower in front of him.

"You guys are busy today," I commented, bending down to help mom with the groceries.

"Well, I was out of a lot of things, so I decided to get the grocery shopping done early and your dad wanted to mow before it got too hot." Smiling at me, she asked, "Do you want to stay for lunch? It won't be much...I just don't seem to have the desire to cook anymore."

"Sure, I'd love to." I helped her put the groceries away and soon we started fixing sandwiches. I noticed mom had lost weight, her cheeks gaunt, but then I realized I had too. Glancing back at dad as he cut off the lawn mower, I noticed the lines on his face deeper and his hair a little whiter. Grief had taken its toll on all of us.

"Mom, where is James' footlocker? The one that the Army sent back?"

She looked over her shoulder and said, "It's up in his old room. Your dad just put it there. We went through it but haven't done anything with any of the contents yet." Her voice shook, but she cleared her throat and continued, "I'll do it when I feel it is the right time. But you're welcome to go through it, sweetie."

Jogging up the stairs, I opened James' old room, finding it much the same as when he left home. Mom had changed his bedspread to one more resembling guest room linens, but it still felt like James was there. Seeing the footlocker at the foot of the bed, I kneeled in front of it and opened the lid. Determined not to cry, I quickly shuffled through his clothes and few personal items, finally finding a few pictures near the bottom. They were of us. *Oh, damn.* I had thought he would have pictures of his Army buddies but I realized that the pictures he had in Afghanistan were of his family. Rubbing my fingers over the image of his smiling face standing next to mine, I sighed. Hearing mom call me for lunch, I replaced the photograph and closed the lid.

Jogging downstairs, I entered the kitchen just as dad walked in through the back door, wiping the sweat from his brow. As his eyes landed on me, his face broke into a huge smile as he enveloped me in a huge bear hug. With his arms around me, I closed my eyes and for a second felt James' arms around me as well.

Dad set me back, still holding onto my hands and asked, "How you doin' baby girl?"

"I'm hanging in there, dad, just like you two."

He pulled me in again and kissed my forehead before walking over to kiss mom. I watched their shared gaze, one of love and understanding. *Oh, how I want that for myself…maybe one day.*

As dad got a glass of water, I sat down on one of the kitchen bar stools. "Mom, dad…I wanted you to know that I've been corresponding with one of James' Army buddies." I watched as they both turned, giving me their full attention. "He wrote condolences to me and we've written back and forth some. I asked him for some tales of James." Giving a little shrug, I added, "I just wanted to know more about James from the past year."

Mom blinked back tears as she gushed, "Oh, Alicia, I think that's wonderful."

Smiling through my own stinging eyes, I nodded. "It's been nice to hear about James from someone who worked and lived with him in the Army." Sucking in a deep breath, I won the battle against the tears and added, "I've also sent him some cookies since I know James shared with his squad."

"Well, let me know the next time you send something and I'll bake some too."

"I'll be sending him a box next week, so if you get them to me, I'll include them."

The three of us sat down to our simple lunch, enjoying each other's company, while secretly wishing James was with us. Four had become three and I wondered if I would ever get used to the change.

★

I HAD JUST gotten on shift at the hospital when the call of an incoming ambulance came in. There were multiple victims and we hurried to be prepared. As the first one unloaded, a small girl was immediately taken back. I stood ready for the next ambulance and as the victim was unloaded, I visibly startled. The young man with dark hair, appearing to be about my age, looked so similar to James. His body had been crushed and partially burned. As the nurses and doctors rushed him back, I moved on wooden legs, my vision blurred with images of James lying there.

We worked non-stop to save him, my training kicking in so I was able to perform my nursing duties on auto-pilot. But our efforts were to no avail and within an hour he died. While the others in the room respectively went about their duties, I stood rooted to the floor, unable to take my eyes off him. I felt a touch on my hand and numbly looked over. Roberta, her eyes full of understanding, said, "Alicia, you need to leave. There's nothing you can do for him now."

Swallowing deeply, I nodded but said, "I just need a

moment."

She stepped back away from me as I walked over to the bed. Looking down, I knew the young man was at peace and in no more pain. I reached out and gently touched his hair, so similar to James', smoothing it back from his face. Closing my eyes, I felt a tear slide unbidden down my cheek, as pain slashed through my heart once more. After I had said a silent prayer for the family that would soon be immersed in the familiar pang of grief, I dashed away my tears and walked back over to the waiting arms of my friend.

"I'm so sorry," Roberta said. "You need to take a break. Get out of here for a bit. Come back when you're ready."

Nodding, I walked out of the ER, no real destination in mind. A few minutes later I found myself standing at the doors to the hospital chapel. Slipping inside the dim interior, I was grateful no one else was present.

Sliding into a pew, I closed my eyes and simply sat for a long time. I was learning that grief can seem to abate and then come roaring back at any moment. I hadn't cried for James in a few weeks, but now the tears flowed freely. For the family of the young man whose life just ended...for our loss of James...*and for Ben.* I thought of his last letter where he talked about his friendship with James. *He's grieving too.* As much as I hated the thought of anyone else hurting, I found comfort in knowing Ben and I shared a similar emotion.

Minutes later I stood, finding a box of tissues at the back of the chapel and dried my tears. Focusing on thoughts of Ben and what I wanted to include in his next package, I sucked in a deep cleansing breath and found renewed strength. Heaving a sigh, I left the peaceful room and made my way back to the ER chaos.

When my shift was over I drove home, exhausted and numb. Skipping dinner, I showered before falling into bed. That night my dreams were dark and twisted. The young man from the ER morphed into James as I tried over and over to save him. Waking suddenly, I kicked the covers off, my body hot and sweaty. Looking at the clock, I saw that it was only three a.m. Knowing sleep would not return soon and not wanting to slip back into nightmares, I got up and padded into the kitchen.

I heated water in the microwave and then plopped in a teabag to steep. Once the cup of tea was ready, I carried it into the living room and sat down on the sofa. Flipping through the channels on the TV, I finally left it on a soft music station as I sipped the hot brew. My thoughts returned to Ben and I wondered what he was doing. I tried to imagine the mechanic's shop where he and James had worked. I tried to imagine their friends. Sitting up quickly, I realized I still had no idea what Ben looked like. Downing the rest of my tea, I moved to the kitchen table, grabbing pen and paper on the way.

Chapter 5

(July – Ben)

THE AFGHANISTAN SUMMER sun beat down on us as we worked in the field. Roger, Jacob, and I were sent on assignment to work on two convoy trucks that had broken down, halting the soldiers' progress. The mountains rose in the background, but out in the inhospitable valley, we felt all too exposed to danger possibly around.

It was only ten a.m. and already over one hundred degrees. Wiping the sweat from my eyes, I buried my head back under the hood of the Oshkosh MTVR.

One of the soldiers standing guard around brought a bottle of water and handed it up to me. "Here you go, man. You'll need this," he offered.

"Appreciate it," I thanked and twisted off the cap. Guzzling half the contents, I pocketed the bottle for later and turned back to my task.

Roger walked over from his vehicle and climbed up beside me. "How's it going?"

"Fuckin' crack allowed sand to collect. I'm trying to get it clean and then we'll need to patch it until they can get the truck back to base for a replacement." My frustration increased along with the heat level. We battled against not only the human enemy, but nature as well. Sand was destroying more engines than IEDs. "What about you?"

"The front differential will need to be replaced but we're getting it patched enough to make it back."

Several hours later, my knuckles were bloodied, grease was embedded underneath my fingernails, and oil stained my uniform. Guzzling one more bottle of water as I jumped back down to the dusty ground, I had the driver turn the engine over once more. Hearing the growl of the truck as it started, I grinned in spite of my fatigue. Roger and Jacob had their vehicle patched by that time and we were ready to head back to base.

With heartfelt thanks from the convoy drivers, we drove away, anxious to get to our destination before dark settled over the land. Breathing a sigh of relief as the base came into view an hour later, we pulled into the gates and made our way toward the machinery garage.

Writing up our report, it took a while for us to finish and by that time, the shift was over. Anxious to get clean, we hustled to the shower tent. For once, the cool water felt amazing as I washed off the sweat and grime. Just like the truck engines, I felt as though the constant wind-blown sand had filled my pores.

Suddenly a thought of James rushed to my mind as I remembered him joking about the sand blowing underneath his uniform and he was afraid of it chafing his dick. Chuckling in spite of my fatigue, I wondered if that was a tale Alicia would like to hear.

Alicia...I hoped to hear from her again soon. For someone I had never met, I looked forward to her letters and hoped mine in return were welcome. James had shown a picture of her to me once and I remembered thinking at the time that she was beautiful. Her smile was infectious and her dark, warm eyes sparkled. The thought of her smile now being gone and her eyes no longer twinkling hit me in the gut. More than anything else, I wanted to make her smile once more.

⭐

STEPPING INTO THE post office, I immediately noticed the grin of the soldier behind the counter.

"Figured you'd be in soon and, gotta tell you, this one's a big one!"

I looked at the large box and matched her grin. "Thanks!" I called out as I carried the box back to the bunks. The tent was half filled and the eyes of my squad took one look at the package and several of them jumped up to see what it contained.

Roger whooped as I opened it and began pulling out bags of treats. "Good God, how much did James' sister send?"

Jacob looked at me speculatively as a slow smile spread across his face. "She's still sending packages?"

Nodding, I avoided his knowing smile and shrugged as I said, "She says she wants to keep taking care of James' former squad." The others appreciated the gesture, but Jacob still eyed me as I passed out the cookies. Seeing the letter in the box, I slid it into my pocket to read later in private.

Being a day off, I soon slipped away easily, walking down the dusty road between the rows of tents. Coming to the Morale, Welfare, and Recreation tent, I stepped inside and found an empty table near the books. Pulling out the letter, I stared for a moment at the familiar handwriting, grinning at the name on the outside. *Ben...not SPC Benjamin Fowler.*

Sliding my finger under the flap, I opened the envelope and pulled out the pages.

Dear Ben,

I hope you are well. As you can see, I've been doing a lot of baking. I guess it's my stress reliever. I'm still having such a hard time and find myself tonight just needing to pour it all out to someone. Lucky you...I guess you'll have to muddle through this with me.

There was a young man who was brought to the ER yesterday and he looked so much like James. But we could not save him and the experience rocked me to my core. All I could think of was James and how he must have suffered. Just when I think I'm getting better, something happens and I cry all over again. Does that happen to you or is that just something that is affecting me?

I do talk to my parents and my closest friend, another nurse named Roberta, but I don't want to burden them. But of course, that's what I'm doing to you, isn't it? I am curious though — does the Army provide any mental health assistance for grief or are soldiers just supposed to "grin and bear it"?

When I went to sleep, I dreamed horrible dreams of James but when I got up, I began to think of you. (don't let that weird you out!) But I wondered how you were and what you were doing.

Are you able to send me any pictures? I know things are probably secure, but I'd love to see the place where you and James worked. And, to be honest, I'd love to see a picture of you as well. I'd like to have a visual of James' friend. And of course, I now count you as a friend also, so I need that picture! If you wonder what I look like, just picture James with no muscles, no facial hair, and dressed like a girl. Oh yeah, and long hair!

Okay, that may have just made me giggle. See? Writing to you helps! I know I could journal write and it might have the same effect, but knowing that someone is on the other end of my letters who knew James makes all the difference.

I'd love to send you more things than just cookies — what do you need the most? (okay, I can't slip a girl into the box!) But seriously, let me know what you all need or can't get there. I've been reading up on what to send but wanted to make sure to include whatever you would like to have.

I know you have mentioned not having any family and I am so sorry about that. If you would like to share, I'd love to know more about you.

By the way, I went to a dinner party the other night at Roberta's house and had to hide in the bathroom for a while. Dr. "I don't know the word no" Simmons cornered me again. But I stayed so long in the bathroom, I may have taken away the "nookie corner" from one of the couples. That's okay — they had other places they could go! But don't worry about me — I can take care of myself! I just thought since James used to share my silly stories, I'd send one to you.

Well, Ben, I feel better. I'll get another package to you soon. Thank you for the gift of not only being James' friend, but now mine as well.

Yours affectionately,
Alicia

I tried to keep my hands from shaking, but was unsuccessful. Scanning the room, I breathed a sigh of relief when I noticed no one was paying any attention to me. My gaze dropped back to the letter in my hands. Something was happening and I was just as unable to stop my emotions as I was stopping my shaking. *Yours affectionately.* Alicia now truly felt like my friend…someone for me to bond with, and not just as James' sister. Scrubbing my hand over my face, I fought those feelings. *She's just being nice. She just needs to connect with someone who knew James. She's just reaching out because of her own grief.* But none of those excuses made a difference to the warmth spreading through my heart.

⭐

THE SHIFT BEFORE us brought in two vehicles, a Humvee and an LMTV cargo truck, both beyond repair. Getting our assignments for the day, we discovered another Humvee had also been brought in that needed parts. Perfect match. Shaking my head, I sometimes wondered if there were any vehicles in all of Afghanistan that weren't rebuilt from the bones of others.

Opening the doors, I began the arduous task of dismantling. For me, I saw it as a chance to save another vehicle…a mechanical organ donor. The sunshine was broken up with clouds today, making the scorcher more bearable. Plus, being inside of the base, our uniforms were lighter, with most of us working in our sand-colored, short-sleeved t-shirts.

Those of us working on dismantling joked amongst ourselves, looking forward to a couple of days off. James, as always, slipped through my mind, knowing how he hated this part of his job. Only this time, instead of slashing me with pain, I began to think of Alicia and my next letter to her. In fact, no matter what I was doing, my thoughts tended to turn toward her. And each time, a goofy smile crossed my face. Looking around quickly, I steeled my expression but noticed Jacob smirking at me. I was grateful that, if he suspected, he kept his mouth shut. The last thing I wanted was for everyone to know I was beginning to have feelings for James' sister.

Chapter 6

(August – Alicia)

"**G**OOD GRIEF, MOM, what on Earth is going on?"

Dad had called and asked if I could come help mom and I hurried over, wondering what she was doing. As soon as I walked into the kitchen, I noticed bags of chocolate chips, flour, eggs, milk, and more baking powder. "What are you baking? Looks like you could feed an Army!"

Mom turned from the counter where she was stirring a large bowl of batter, and grinned. "Guilty."

"Huh?" Then I realized what I had said and clarified, "So you are trying to feed the whole Army?"

She tucked her hair behind her ear, smearing some flour on her cheek and said, "I've joined the local chapter of the American Gold Star Mothers. Thankfully, there's not too many of us, but I'm also in the Blue Star Mothers chapter."

Mom had joined the Blue Star Mothers when James first joined the service, but I knew her participation had waned after he died. "Gold Star Mothers?" I asked.

"It's also a veterans' service organization, but it's mothers who have lost a son or daughter in the service." Her smile was sad, but I saw a brightness in her eyes that had been missing for months.

"Do you have a project going?" I wondered aloud.

Nodding, mom smiled softly, also the first I had seen in months. "Yes, we're baking for care packages to send to the troops."

I observed her closely, her grief still raw, but the determination to help others still very real. Remembering Ben's words about James wanting to help others, I smiled knowing where he inherited the trait.

Looking at the baking supplies still on the counter, I said, "Thinking about the Blue Star moms doing care packages makes me think that I should send more than just cookies. Maybe I'll do some for his squad and include other things as well. You'll have to let me know what to put in it."

"That would be lovely!" mom exclaimed, while dad simply smiled. "I'll put their squad up for our group to send packages to as well."

The three of us got busy with mom and me baking and dad looking up lists of things soldiers needed. He blushed and said, "I know what we used to send James but I'm finding lists for female soldiers as well. I'll print these out and you can go shopping, Alicia."

"You don't want to go, dad?" I teased.

Gaining the reaction I knew was coming, dad shuddered. "Me? At Walmart? Hell, no!"

Mom and I shared a look then burst into giggles as dad continued. "That store may have everything, but I get lost and walk for miles just trying to find men's underwear!"

At that, we all laughed, my heart feeling lighter. "Okay, dad, you do the lists and I'll do the shopping." With him readily agreeing, I felt re-energized for the first time in months.

★

THIS TIME THE envelope with Ben's handwriting on it was much thicker than normal. Giddy with excitement, I threw my purse down, kicked off my clogs, and plopped down on the sofa with my feet on the coffee table. Tiger jumped up and settled down on my lap, in our now usual letter-reading pose.

Ripping open the envelope, several pictures fell from between the pages. Snatching them greedily, my heart pounded as I savored a photograph of James and several other soldiers standing in a large room with trucks behind them and mechanic's tools scattered at their feet. The five men stood side by side with their arms around each other, huge smiles on their faces. I sought out James first, the familiar dark hair so like my own and his handsome face pierced my heart. He looked so happy...so carefree with his friends doing the job he loved to do. But no tears came. This time I simply viewed him as he was and felt glad that if he had been so far from home, at least he was surrounded by his squad.

My gaze was then drawn to the man on the end next to James, the two of them taller than the others. This soldier's brown hair was not as dark as James but neatly trimmed in his military cut. His t-shirt was stretched across his chest and his muscular biceps were showing. His handsome face held a bit of a boyish grin, as though one of them had just cracked a dirty joke. *I wonder...*

Flipping the picture over, I saw their names. And right next to James was listed Ben Fowler. My smile widened. Looking at the next two pictures, I saw a candid shot that was a close up of a group of soldiers playing cards. The two men facing the camera were James and Ben. *They both look happy.* Somehow that thought gave me courage. The last picture was just of Ben and on the back it said, **Alicia, Thanks for your friendship. Ben**

My heart lighter than it had been in ages, I slid deeper into the sofa as I opened the letter.

Dear Alicia,

Your last package was amazing and so appreciated

by all! I know you want to send more things but I don't want you to feel obligated. Honestly, I'm okay, but we can always use toiletries and stuff like that.

I was glad you told me about your dreams and even about the young man from the ER. I don't know how you do your job – you are amazing to be a nurse in such a stressful environment. It's a true gift. But it is important for you to take care of yourself as well. I know James would want that for you, and if you don't mind my saying, I want that for you also.

I hope you like the pictures. I found two that had James in them and I know you wanted to see him in his workplace. The group photo was taken when we first got here and poker night was just about a month before he died. I also included one of me—you can throw it away if you want, but I figured you should see who you're writing to. I saw a picture of you with James a long time ago, but I'd like to have more than just the memory of that one and the hilarious visual you presented in your last letter! So please send one for me if you don't mind.

You asked about my family but there's not much to tell. My mom was a single mom after my dad left us. I was only a baby so I don't remember him. He was never part of my life, but mom did the best she could. She had a longtime boyfriend who owned a garage and he taught me all about cars and engines. I used to love hanging out there and soaking up everything I could. Mom died when I was only fifteen and since she and Oscar never married, he had no legal claim on me. I was sent to a foster home but it was hard to adjust. I'm afraid I didn't make it easy on them and ended up being shuffled to about four more foster homes until I finally turned eighteen. I joined the Army on my eighteenth birthday and never looked back.

I got the MOS I wanted, which was Wheeled Vehicle Mechanic. There are other types of mechanics from tracked vehicles, Stryker systems, helicopter, artillery, to Bradley vehicles, but if it's got wheels, I knew I could learn to fix it. I just never knew how many different kinds of wheeled vehicles the military used until I was trained. Like James didn't, I don't want to spend my whole career in the Army. In fact, I plan on getting out of the service after this tour is over with. I've got five more months to go. I should be able to get a job in a garage but I'd ultimately like to own one myself. That's down the road, but still a goal.

Do you want to stay an ER nurse? By the way, while your Dr. Simmons' story was amusing, I think he may need me to talk to him when I get out! If that asshole keeps bothering you, I will be paying him a visit! And this is not because I owe it to James to look after you, but because I want to.

Well, I guess that's enough for now. I'll include my email in case you ever want to write to me that way. It's quicker, but then I don't want to give up my goodie boxes! It's really sweet of you to take the time to do this and even though I know you say it's good for you to do when you think about James, it's still nice for you to send them. I wish I had something I could send to you as a thank-you, but there's not much here that I think you would want. Anyway, take care and write soon.

I really look forward to your letters - and don't forget about a picture!

Love,

Ben

My heart stuttered as I looked at the signature. *Love, Ben.* I knew it was a throw-away signature and it didn't mean anything, but it still filled me with warmth. I picked up the three pictures again, my fingers gingerly tracing over James' face in two of them and then holding Ben's picture carefully. He looked like the kind of man who could walk into a party and women would flock to him. Sighing, I wondered if that was what he was used to.

Standing, I went to the storage closet in the hall and dug around in some boxes. Finding what I was looking for, I took out the three picture frames I had bought on sale months ago and placed the pictures in each. Moving back to my mantle, I set the group picture there and then, moving to my bedroom, I placed the poker game picture of James and Ben as well as the single picture of Ben on my nightstand. *Perfect.* They will be the last thing I look at when I go to bed and the first thing I look at when I wake up. I knew it was dangerous, but my heart was beginning to be more involved with Ben than my head thought was a good idea.

The next morning, I rose early and drove to Walmart

armed with the list from my dad on what soldiers in the field need. I started with the toiletries, going to the travel-size section. I piled in the shampoos, body wash, razors, shaving creams, lotion, sunscreen, hand sanitizer, antiseptic cream, Band-aids, tissues, foot powder, and feminine products. *I need to ask him if there are women mechanics in his squad.* This thought actually sent a jolt through me...*I wonder if he's involved with someone?* Heaving a sigh, I continued shopping, pushing that thought out of my mind. I'll just have to ask him next time.

Moving to the clothing section, I loaded my cart with cotton socks and underwear. *Oh Jesus, what if he thinks I'm crazy sending underwear?* Once more shaking that idea from my mind, I focused on the task at hand, refusing to overthink the process.

Next, I moved to the food section and grabbed protein bars, candy, gum, and packets of nuts. Then I added cocoa and fruit-flavored drink mixes. My list included things that the service members can use to make their food more palatable, so I added some flavor spice packets, a few jars of barbecue sauce, mustard, and ketchup.

By now, my large cart was filled to the brim and I eyed it dubiously. *How will I ever mail all this?* Refusing to allow doubts about my endeavors to creep in, I marched toward the register and closed my eyes as the total was rung up. As the cashier called out the amount, I was pleasantly surprised. Breathing a sigh of relief, I slid my credit card and proceeded to load the bags back into the cart.

Once home, I rounded up several boxes, knowing not everything could go in a single container. Tiger was excited about the activity, deciding to help. Jumping in one box and then another, she finally settled on the floor and batted the small toiletry bottles around the room.

Laughing, I snagged them away from her and placed the toiletries in plastic bags so if there was leakage, it would not get all over the whole box. I had my iPod in the speakers, listening to country music as I worked. My heart lighter as I carefully packed the rest of the items. By the time I was finished, I had four boxes to mail. Smiling as I adhered a mailing label to each one, I stood back and admired my work.

Feeling an ease I had not felt in a long time, I heated a cup of tea. As it steeped, I walked into my bedroom and grabbed the framed picture of Ben from my nightstand and carried it back with me. Setting it on the kitchen table next to my tea, I sat down to write. Peering at his smiling face as I wrote, I felt closer to him.

Chapter 7

(September – Ben)

IT'S PARTY TIME. Roger's tour is up and tonight is his last night, so we've decided to live it up. And the timing could not be more perfect.

Yesterday, I got four boxes from Alicia and the squad was thrilled. With four boxes, I had to get help carrying them back to our tent and, even though my name was on the outside, the guys jumped into the parcels. And one of them pulled out a note saying, **Ben, I hope you enjoy all the goodies. Be sure to share! Alicia**

Much to my surprise, they were cool about her sending packages to me. Breathing a sigh of relief, I dug into the boxes, pulling out the booty. *Jesus, did she buy all of this herself?* We pulled out bags of toiletries, cracked a few jokes about the feminine products, but knew we had fellow female soldiers that would be thrilled with them. The socks and underwear were a bonus as well. We used one of the boxes as a future storage kit and filled it with the medicines and Band-aids.

But for our impromptu party, the food items were a

hit. *She has no idea how perfect this is!* We didn't have alcohol on our base but it was not missed with the flavor packets we added to bottles of water. We confiscated a corner of the DFAC and with the extra condiments and spices, we had a feast.

Taking the chicken that was served and added taco seasoning, we made the flavor go from mild to wild. Roger, drinking a grape drink, laughed, "I haven't had Kool-Aid since I was a kid! This stuff is great!" The meal was topped off with some of Alicia's chocolate chip cookies. I grinned as I looked around at the group and for the first time the pang of not having James in the middle of us was lessened. *Thanks to his sister.*

The next morning, we said goodbye to Roger, each of us thinking of when it would be our turn. Most of us came on tour to Afghanistan together but a few of the mechanics transferred in at different times. I looked toward Jacob and held up four fingers indicating four more months. He nodded and grinned. We actually had already filled out the paperwork for the Transition Assistance Program and were counting down the days. Lately, I had to admit, I wondered if there would be the chance for me to meet Alicia when I got back stateside. *Who am I kidding? I'd like a lot more than just an opportunity to meet!*

Sighing heavily, I turned to walk back to the garage when Jacob jogged up beside me. Slapping me on the back, he said, "Okay, spill."

Looking sideways in surprise, I reared back. "Spill? Spill what?"

"About you and James' sister."

Throwing my hands up, I started to protest, but looking into his face knowing he had grieved for James as well, I finally just said, "We're...pen pals."

Jacob's eyebrows lifted as he barked out a laugh. "Come on, man. This is me you're talking to. I can tell there's a lot more going on than just being pen pals."

We made it to the garage in silence and I had the feeling he was allowing me the silence to gather my thoughts. Settling in to work on one of the trucks I was assigned to, my mind was on the beautiful brunette sending the care packages. Jacob didn't pressure me, but I had to admit part of me wanted to talk to someone about what was going on...or what I wish was going on.

Standing up, wiping the grease from my hands, I looked over at him and said, "I guess the easiest thing to say is that after James died, I wrote her a condolence letter. James had always read her letters to us and I just wanted her to know how much we were going to miss him, but I also wanted to make sure she knew how much she meant to him."

Jacob nodded slowly, his lips curved slightly. "I never thought of doing that, man. That was a really nice thing to do for her."

Shrugging, I added, "You know I never had much family to talk about and sure as shit don't now...so I guess I was always envious of the relationship he had with his sister. I thought it was really cool and I figured she was grieving and maybe needed to hear that we were too."

He was silent for a moment, his face thoughtful before lifting his gaze back to me. "And then?"

"She wrote back and thanked me. Said it was nice to talk to someone who knew James here. She asked if I would share a few stories about him. So we began to write back and forth. We've emailed occasionally but since she usually sends a box, we generally send letters."

I turned my attention back to the engine and continued to work on the truck. Jacob had gotten quiet so I figured the topic was closed. He surprised me when he asked, "What about now? I get the feeling it's a lot more. And you're going home in four months."

I cut my eyes over to him and said, "Seriously? She's an ER nurse with doctors wanting to date her. What the hell does this grease monkey have to offer someone like her?"

His face registered shock as his mouth fell open. "If you really believe that then you're a total dumbass! Jesus, Ben...her twin brother was a mechanic. Same as you. You already know she was proud of him. Do you really think she cares if you're one also?"

I hadn't thought about that and felt the heat rise on my face as he continued.

"Sounds to me like you two have some kind of bond that you share. Whether it stemmed from James' death or not, by now it's real. And you'd be an idiot to pass up the opportunity to see if it goes beyond being a pen pal!"

Facing Jacob again, I hesitated giving voice to another one of my fears. Seeing him waiting, his impatience growing, I blurted, "What would James think about it?"

His frown eased into sympathy as he slowly shook his head and said, "Man, James was your best friend. I mean, he and I were good friends, but you two had one of those great friendships that, if he had lived, would have lasted forever." Chuckling, he added, "The two of you were getting out at the same time and you know he would have had you go home with him. You'd have met his sister at some point because he would have had you over to his house all the time."

I stared at him, having never thought of that either, but he wasn't finished.

"James loved his sister, probably more than anything or anybody. And he cared for you. I have a feeling he would haved loved for you two to hook up. Hell, he might have even tried to arrange it."

The tight band around my heart loosened as I listened to Jacob talk about James and Alicia. Letting out a deep sigh, I grinned. "Maybe you're right."

"Fuck yeah, I'm right!" he exclaimed, moving over to the next truck in line.

I went back to work on the motor, my tangled thoughts slowly unraveling. Memories of conversations with James, that I had buried along with him, slid back to the forefront of my mind. James used to tell me his sister needed someone like me. Or talk about how he and I could get out of the Army and open a mechanics shop together. He would talk about having me come over to his mom's house for Sunday dinners.

My heart lighter, I continued to work as I mentally counted down the days until I could meet Alicia.

★

"JUST A LETTER today…guess that seems measly, doesn't it?" the post officer Private called out. In her hand was an envelope with Alicia's distinctive handwriting.

Grinning, I shook my head. "Nope, this is like hitting the jackpot every time," I confessed.

"It must be love," she joked, startling me as I accepted the letter from her.

Walking outside, the sun still baking the base, I decided to go back to the bunks, which were typically empty this time of day. I plopped down on my bed and leaned back against the headboard. Opening the letter, I unfolded the pages and my finger landed on a picture.

My breath caught in my throat as I flipped it over and viewed Alicia's face. I remembered seeing her picture with James a long time ago, but my memory was nothing compared to what I was staring at now. Long, dark brown hair hung below her shoulders, gentle waves framing her face. Her chocolate eyes twinkled as her rosy lips curved in a wide, slightly crooked smile. *Damn, James had the exact same smile!*

My heart pounded as I traced her face. Propping it on my chest, I began to read.

Dear Ben,

I hope you got the boxes of goodies I sent. I had such a good time shopping for you (and the squad). I didn't know if there were any female mechanics (I guess you know by now, I sent some "girl things"). You can just give them to anyone who can use them.

You and James had a shared love of fixing cars — we had an uncle that always tinkered with old cars and James used to spend hours with him from the time he could stand on a step-stool and peek under a hood! I think you would have an easy time getting a job back here as a mechanic.

You asked about nursing — I've always wanted to be a nurse, since I was little. I always pretended that my dolls got sick or hurt and I would make them better. In nursing school, I decided that I like the fast pace of the ER, but after a couple of years, I confess to burning out a little bit. I might look for another nursing job sometime, but for now the money is good.

Thank you for sharing about your family in your last letter. I'm so sorry for the loss of your mom. I can't imagine how hard that must have been. But James always spoke so highly of you, and now that I've gotten to know you, I can certainly tell you that your mom would be proud of you.

I realized that I don't know where you are from. What state did you grow up in? Will you go back there when you get out of the Army? I've lived in the Virginia Beach area my whole life. Mom and dad still have the house that James and I were raised in.

Speaking of mom, she belonged to the Blue Star Mothers, a service group of moms of servicemen and women. Now she also has joined the American Gold Star Mothers, a group for moms who have lost a child in service. It's been good for her and she's started doing projects with them. Mom and dad helped me with the things that I sent to you.

I'd really like for you to meet my parents when you get out. To be honest, I'd really love to meet you in person as well. Any chance you could come to Virginia when you leave Afghanistan?

I've never asked if you have a girlfriend. You know all about my disastrous love life — or lack thereof, but I know nothing about yours. To be honest, I've given up on dating for now.

I hope you like the picture. I always think I

look weird in photographs (James and I shared a "wonky" smile — mom said it was because we were so squished inside of her, but our grandmother had the same smile!) Anyway, this picture was one where I thought I looked okay.

I have now reached the point where I can think or talk about James and not tear up. I know that grief is a journey and I have to follow my own path, but I never knew how hard it would be. But you have helped me so much — you have no idea how often I think of you and instantly I'm lifted from my sad thoughts. You truly are a very special person, Ben, and I count myself lucky to know you.

Well, it looks like my letters are getting longer, so I'll close for now. Please think about coming to Virginia when you get out. I truly would love to see you in person.

Love,
Alicia

I picked up her picture and stared at it again, memorizing each feature, now that her words were in my head—and if I was honest, her words were implanted in my heart.

This was her longest letter and as my gaze roamed over it again, I knew we shared something special. I rested my head against my pillow and closed my eyes for a moment. I'd never known anyone like her...so completely giving. A small smile slid onto my face as I realized that she was actually the second person who gave so much of themselves…James was the first.

I re-read the last couple of paragraphs again and my smile widened. She thinks I'm special. She wants to meet me. And right then, I vowed my first stop in the states would be Virginia.

Chapter 8

(October – Alicia)

*D*O I WANT *to stay in the ER?* This thought rattled around my brain for weeks. I'd never spent a lot of time thinking about it but ever since Ben asked if this was where I wanted to stay, I couldn't get the question out of my mind.

The duties of an ER nurse that I loved when I first graduated from nursing school, were now things that I didn't like. The pace gave me no time to actually get to know a patient. The long shifts gave me little time for anything else. The staff was professional and dedicated, but I no longer loved my job. Sighing, I set my now-empty tea mug into the sink as I began my day off. Looking around, I decided my house was desperate for a cleaning, plus the mindless task gave me plenty of time to think. Throwing myself into the picking up, dusting, vacuuming, and scrubbing the bathrooms and kitchen, I contemplated the pros and cons of the ER.

Two hours later, my home was clean but I was no

closer to deciding on my career path. Sighing as I put away my supplies, I looked at the time. Mom was having a Blue Star Mother meeting and I'd promised to have lunch with her afterward. Jumping into the shower, I quickly got ready.

Later, sitting in the little restaurant with mom, I looked over at her and smiled. Her face was more relaxed...her eyes a little brighter.

"You look good, mom," I murmured, reaching out to touch her hand.

A sad smile crossed her lips and she squeezed my fingers. "I'm trying, baby girl. Each day...a step at a time."

"Tell me what your group is working on," I prompted.

"Right now, we're in the process of getting a work crew together to do holiday boxes that we'll be sending from mid-November through the end of December. We have almost one hundred volunteers so far and we're already accepting donations."

"What can I do to help?"

"Oh, Alicia, you're already doing so much for James' old squad," she protested.

Shrugging, I said, "I can always do more. I can make sure to ask for a day off when you all are packing the boxes."

Her warm smile beamed on me as she nodded.

"That'd be wonderful, honey. We'll have our packing day in about a month and the Hampton Veterans Medical Center is providing a large room for us to use that day."

I tilted my head to the side as I thought of what she just said. "Hampton Veterans Medical Center? Why haven't I heard of that?"

"From what I understand it's a full-service hospital serving the veterans." Mom scrunched her forehead as she added, "I think they have a couple of outpatient locations as well. In fact, I'm pretty sure one of them is in Virginia Beach and another in Chesapeake."

"Hmmm," I said, my curious mind already mulling over the work of these facilities. Saying nothing to mom, I decided to check into them.

Jolting, I realized she had asked a question and I'd missed it. "I'm sorry, what did you ask?"

"I was just wondering if you were still corresponding with that soldier friend of James'?"

I felt a blush creep over my face and hoped that she missed seeing it. I should have known that wouldn't happen. Before I had a chance to formulate my answer, she laughed.

"I see that you must still be in contact with him, and if that blush is any indication, you are enjoying that contact!"

Blushing brighter, I rolled my eyes. "Oh, mom, you

make me sound like a teenager," I complained, but had trouble keeping the smile off my face. "Okay, I admit, Ben and I are still corresponding and I really like what I'm learning about him."

She patted my hand and said, "James was a giving person but he was also discriminating when it came to his friends. That, in and of itself, tells me Ben is a good man as well as a good soldier."

"I confess I really like him, mom, but I know that's premature. I'm sure he just thinks of me as a good friend."

"When does he get back from tour?"

"I think in about three months."

Smiling again, mom said, "Well, once he's back, maybe you can meet in person."

Nodding, I didn't tell her I had already invited him to come. Now I just had to wait for his next letter.

★

Dear Alicia,

You cannot imagine the excitement your boxes brought to the squad! We divided up the toiletries and yes, there are a few women mechanics and they were appreciative of your gifts for them. The guys teased me, but I put them in a box and handed them to one of our female mechanics and just said, "Here, my friend sent these for any women here." Then I'm sure I blushed as I walked away. I know, I know…men are such wimps when it comes to those products!

Laughing out loud at the vision of handsome Ben, blushing as he mumbled his way through handing a box of sanitary products to a female soldier, I was glad they were shared with those who needed them.

It was nice to hear you talk about James and how much he loved being a mechanic. That shows me you understand my fascination with the same career. I know I'm not college educated, but I love what I can fix with my own two hands. And as far as your nursing goes, keep doing what makes you happy but don't be afraid of change. My life has had lots of changes and some of them have opened up amazing opportunities.

I know what you mean about being able to handle thinking of James a little easier now. For a long time, his loss hammered me, whether I was working on a five-ton truck, dismantling a Humvee, or just playing a game of cards with him not here. Men, especially soldiers, are supposed to be such bad-asses, but the pain of losing my best friend killed me. But, I can think of him now without that punch to the gut. And most of that is due to you, Alicia. I hope you know how important you have become to me. (I hope that did not sound too needy - I don't want to scare you away!)

I'm from a little town in rural Pennsylvania, but I've got no ties there now. I admit I was thrilled that you would like me to meet your parents. And, to be honest, I was really excited at the prospect of meeting you. I've got nowhere special to be when I leave the military and would love to come and visit. I've got a few more pictures of James and me that I would be honored to share with your mom and dad, if you think that would be appropriate.

You asked if I had a girlfriend and the answer is a definite No! I've had a few relationships in the past, but they never lasted long. I confess that when you said you were giving up on dating for a while, I grinned. Alicia, I'm going out on a limb and will just say that I've got a lot of changes coming up in the next couple of months. I rotate back home in two months, have a month of transition and then will be out of the Army. I'll have to figure out where to live and then find a job. The Army will help but I've heard there's only so much they can do. Most of it will be up to me. Who knows? I might look in Virginia for a mechanic job.

There are a lot of things I'm excited about doing again. Like going to Walmart, eating in a restaurant or even getting a McDonalds' hamburger. I want to take a shower that can last for more than a couple of minutes. I want to buy a pickup truck. I want to go to the beach and swim in the ocean. I want to find a nice, green park and just run in the grass. I even want to rent a mountain cabin and watch it snow.

But the thing that I am most excited about is meeting you. More than anything. If you're not dating anyone then, I'd love to take you to dinner. And a movie. I haven't thanked you for your picture yet, but you should know that I look at it every day and cannot wait until I can see you in *person. Your picture is beautiful but it is nothing compared to the beauty on the inside of you. Just know that James would be so proud of you.*

I'll close for now, but the hope that in about three months I can see you in person will get me through the last weeks here in this place.

Love,

Ben

I clutched the letter to my chest as a tear slid down my face. Ben had slowly crept into my life and had become so important to me, but I feared I was just a pen pal to him. This letter gave me hope that he was feeling the same.

Opening my eyes, I placed the pages on my lap and smoothed them with my fingers. I glanced over at the calendar I kept on my refrigerator and headed into the kitchen, grabbing a marker on my way. I didn't know the exact date he would be getting out, but I knew it had to be in January. Counting from the middle of January back, I began writing a Ben-gets-out countdown on each day of the calendar. Less than eighty days!

★

HALLOWEEN IN THE ER…worst place ever.

Four emergencies with children who had nut allergies and had eaten candy with peanuts. Five cases of children being hit by cars while out trick-or-treating. Three burn cases from lighting candles in the Jack-O-Lanterns. And that didn't even include the adults who were dressed in costumes, drank too much, and ended up in fights, accidents, or just plain stupid injuries.

One of the final ones of the evening was a young man brought in by ambulance with the police in attendance. He was in full Army ACU, with blood all over his chest. The EMTs called out he had been stabbed in a bar fight. The wound was superficial but would need to be stitched.

I stood to the side, rooted in place, shaking as I stared down at him. Lifting my gaze to the policeman, I asked, "Is he an active duty soldier or a veteran?"

"Huh?"

"This soldier? Is he active duty or a veteran at home?"

"Neither...this is just a costume. He was at some Halloween party at one of the local bars."

I began to shake with anger as I stared at the man on the table. "A costume?" I yelled. "When real soldiers are dying, he's wearing a fuc—"

Roberta shoved me to the side, saying, "Go, get out of here. We've got this. Take a break." When I didn't move, she got in between me and the vision of the fake soldier and said, "Alicia—go now, honey. You don't need to see this."

Blinking out of my furious stupor, I nodded and turned, blindly stumbling down the hall. Other ER personnel were seeing to his wounds and I wasn't needed, which was good because, at that moment, I would have been more likely to pummel him than treat him.

I made it to the nurses' lounge before bursting into tears. Falling into a chair, I sobbed...for James...for my parents whose pain would never heal...for Ben and the others who were still in danger. After several long minutes, my tears finally slowed. I grabbed some napkins from the table and wiped my face, sucking in a shuddering breath. I glanced up at the clock and realized my shift was almost over.

Over. That's how this felt. Truly over.

Roberta opened the door and slipped inside, sitting next to me and pulling me close. "I'm sorry, Alicia. Why don't you go on home?"

Nodding, I turned to look at her. "I'm going to check out the nursing jobs available at one of the VA hospitals in the area." As I said the words out loud to her that I had not verbalized to myself, I realized they were true...and needed.

Being the good friend that she was, she didn't try to talk me out of it. She just smiled sadly and nodded. Maybe she knew before I did, that it was time for a change.

Chapter 9

(November – Ben)

THANKSGIVING CAME AND, this year, for the first time in years, I had a lot to be thankful for. And the beautiful brunette with the slightly crooked smile and generous spirit waiting to meet me back in the states was at the top of my list.

The DFAC did a good job with Thanksgiving, but the next box from Alicia made it even better with the seasoning packets and cans of cranberry sauce and gravy. The squad ate together and our spirits were high. Four of us would be transferring out in early January and the rest would go in a few months after that.

A chill was in the air but it felt good after the hotter-than-hell summer months. Looking forward to being back in the states soon when it was cold and snowy was exciting.

"What's the first thing you gonna do when you get back?" Brett called out.

"Get drunk and get laid...but not necessarily in that

order!" Sam yelled out, to the laughter of the others.

Shaking my head, I looked up, seeing the others staring at me. A quip came to mind but suddenly I had no desire to lie or brag. Shrugging, I said, "Guess I'll head to Virginia and meet up with James' family." The jocularity left the group and I felt guilty about that. "Come on, guys. That's a good thing. I'll spend some time with them, share some stories, and make sure to thank Alicia for her generosity."

Slow smiles filled the table and I braced for their teasing, but was pleasantly surprised. "Well, give her our thanks as well, man," Paul, one of the newer squad members, said.

Later Jacob and I were walking out together when he said, "You know, just because it's been long-distance, you and Alicia share something really special. I wish you two the best."

Grinning, I nodded, completely agreeing. Less than fifty days to go.

★

Dear Ben,

You didn't give me the date of when you get back, but I've been doing a calendar countdown anyway and hope I'm not too far off! I can't wait to meet you in person!

I realized the other night that, other than my

parents and my friend, Roberta, I think you know me better than anyone. Mom and dad definitely want you to come see them and they would love to see any pictures you have of James and any stories you can share. I know it will be after the holidays but it will be the best Christmas present.

Speaking of the holidays, I know this will be the most difficult one for us. I think we'll keep it kind of easy – I thought about having my parents come to my apartment so they won't have to face their house without James this year.

I wanted to tell you my latest news – I am looking at changing jobs. My mom and I were at the Hampton Veterans Medical Center, which is a full hospital, (we were packing up boxes to send to soldiers for the holidays) and I really like their facility. I went to talk to the head of nursing and she said they had openings. I'm going back this week to take a tour and complete my application. I would not be working in emergency, but am looking to be in their post-surgical unit. Well, either that or their rehabilitation services. The time is right...I need a change and you've given me the encouragement to do what's right for me. Thank you for that!

I hope I'm not being too presumptuous, but I can't wait to take you to Walmart and McDonalds! And I would definitely accept your invitation to dinner and a movie! By the time you get this letter, it won't be long at all. So excited!!

Please take care of yourself and expect to get at least one more box of goodies (Christmas cookies this time!) See you soon!

Love,
Alicia

Grinning, the thoughts of taking Alicia to dinner filled my mind. Hell, even the idea of wandering the aisles of Walmart sharing a shopping cart with her made my head spin.

"Hey, Fowler!"

I shoved Alicia's letter back into my pocket and threw my lunch trash into the bin. "Yeah?" I called out to Jacob.

"Got a call for a re-claim. Looks like it's you and me."

Nodding, I went to get suited up. Our Staff Sergeant came over to give us the information that we would have an armed escort, due to the fighting that had recently been going on in the area.

Within thirty minutes, we were in our armored five-ton wrecker in the middle of the escort convoy. We turned and headed up toward the mountains, the opposite direction from where I'd been before. The terrain became rougher and rockier, but our M1089 crunched over the gravel as we made our way. Coming upon the overturned vehicle, I let out a sigh of relief, seeing the job would not be difficult.

Maneuvering our wrecker, we made fast work of attaching the winch lines. Once inside, we pulled it over, back on its wheels. Jacob got out again as I maneuvered the wrecker to get into the right position to hook up the towing mechanisms.

Suddenly the sound of rapid gunfire echoed off the cliffs around us and our escort immediately returned fire. Jerking around, I looked for Jacob but couldn't find him. A Sergeant pounded on my window, and yelled, "Go! We're pushing out!"

"Specialist Balston's still out there!"

The Sergeant ducked down and within a minute came back covering Jacob. As he climbed back in the armored cab we got our orders to drive on, the convoy would follow.

Putting the wrecker in gear, I started down the road. Glancing to the side, I asked, "You okay, man?"

"Yeah," Jacob replied, his voice hoarse with adrenaline. "I got some rounds off but fucking hell, Ben, I'm glad the escort was with us."

Nodding, I agreed, my heart pounding as the sounds of gunfire continued all around. Looking in my side view mirrors, I saw some of the armored vehicles of the convoy falling in line behind us and one was coming up alongside, soon to pass in front. As we bumped along the rocky terrain down the mountain side, we slowly made our way back to base. As the sounds of conflict disappeared, I breathed a sigh of relief.

Now that I had someone to get home to, I wanted nothing to interfere. Pulling through the base gates as the sun was setting, we made our way to the garage. Our squad was waiting for us, having heard about the attack. Assuring them we were fine, they assisted with unhooking the towed vehicle. Completing the paperwork in record time, Jacob and I headed off to the showers.

★

As I OPENED the package from Alicia, I knew this would be the last care package I would get from her. It wasn't large, but it did hold a surprise. There was just one baggie of her chocolate chip cookies, but also an envelope filled with papers. It didn't appear to be a letter but as I opened it, I sucked in a breath realizing what I was looking at. Pages of computer printouts of mechanic job openings in the Hampton Roads area of Virginia. *Alicia has done a ton of research into a new job for me already...this must mean she wants me to live nearby!*

Unable to keep the grin off my face, I perused the job openings she had listed while munching a cookie.

Jacob poked his head into the tent and called out, "Ben, Sarge wants to see us."

I looked up in surprise. "Now?"

"Yep. You, me, Mendez, and Toller."

He and I shared a look, recognizing the four he

wanted to talk to were the four who were supposed to leave for the States from tour in about six weeks. My stomach felt punched as I wondered why we were being called in. After all, the needs of the Army take precedence over everything.

Jacob and I hustled to the garage, meeting up with the other two mechanics, their expressions just as surprised and worried as ours.

Chapter 10

(December – Alicia)

"**M**S. NEWTON, WE are very pleased to have you join our staff."

I walked down the hall with Donna Perkins, the head of the nursing department at the Hampton Veterans Medical Center. Holiday decorations were hung over the doors and in the glass windows.

"We have a long and proud history," she continued. "In 1865, Abraham Lincoln authorized the first national soldiers' and sailors' asylum to provide medical care for discharged members of the Union Army and Navy forces. This is the fourth one in the nation to be developed. It's been operating for 135 years."

Impressed, I nodded, taking it all in. "I can't tell you how excited I am to be here," I freely admitted.

Donna smiled at me and said, "You'll find the pace here much slower than the ER, but from what you told me, that won't be a problem."

"No, ma'am. I loved the ER for a long time, but I

missed having a relationship with my patients. And after my brother was killed, I was made so aware of the families of our veterans that have needs. I'm excited to be working with both the wounded veterans and their families."

Nodding, she patted my shoulder as we continued to walk throughout the large facility. We ended up in the surgical area where I was introduced to the other nurses on staff that day. Providing post-op care was just what I had requested.

I thanked her profusely as I began my first shift, knowing the change was the best decision for me. As I was taken on a tour of the post-op floor, I noticed a large wall calendar and grinned as I thought of my calendar at home with my countdown to Ben clearly marked.

Forcing thoughts of him out of my mind, I smiled at the charge nurse as we began the day.

✮

I SHOULD HAVE known Christmas Eve would hurt.

Mom and dad agreed to spend Christmas with me in my little house, so I spent the day before decorating. With a wreath on the door and a small tree in the corner, I hung ornaments on its branches. Mom loaned me the family ornaments for this year and I found the ones James and I had made each year in elementary school.

Heaving a sigh, I wondered how we would get through the day. Tiger, excited with the decorations, stood on her hind legs and batted at the tree. I smiled, glad for the distraction.

Mom was bringing a ham and an apple pie and I was providing the side dishes. We had all bought simple gifts this year for us to open. I knew dad would open some wine and we'd listen to Christmas music. *We'll get through the day together…just like we always do.*

I looked at the clock and made a last minute decision. Slipping into my coat and boots, I grabbed my purse and walked down the street to a small neighborhood church. Just as the Christmas Eve service was beginning, I slid into a pew. The candles provided soft illumination as the organist played Silent Night.

Closing my eyes, I felt peace moving through me. James would no longer be walking beside me, but his spirit would always be at my side. A tear snaked down my cheek and I brushed it away just as the choir began to sing a medley of Christmas hymns.

An hour later, I stepped out of the church and looked up in surprise as a light snow began to fall, creating a magical snow-globe view of my world. My heart lighter, I hurried home to finish the preparations for mom and dad's visit tomorrow.

⭐

I LAUGHED AT the expression on dad's face when he opened one of his gifts from his eccentric sister—a gift certificate to a local spa.

"What the hell am I going to do with this?" he chuckled.

"Oh Lordy, George," mom exclaimed, "I think she got our gifts mixed up." Mom held up a Craftsman tool set. "This is what she gave me!"

Mom and dad sat on the sofa next to each other and I had to admit they had done very well, although mom teared up when she saw my tree with the childhood decorations. But over coffee and monkey-bread we talked about James and Christmases past. Opening presents to the sounds of Christmas music on the TV made for a relaxing morning.

Later, dad piled up on the sofa with Tiger in his lap while mom and I retreated to my small kitchen to heat lunch. I stirred the yams while mom pulled the ham from the oven. I watched as mom took a beer to dad and his eyes left the TV, his face breaking into a soft smile as she approached. Patting his lap, she sat down and he wrapped his arms around her, tucking her in tightly.

I blinked rapidly as I observed their love. It lasted through what no parents should have to do...bury a child. I gripped the counter unable to take my eyes off them as dad wiped the few tears from my mom's cheeks before she leaned in to kiss him. Sharing a small smile, mom stood up squeezing his hand before walking away.

Swallowing deeply, I turned quickly and continued to place dishes on the counter. Mom walked in behind and wrapped her arms around me. "Love you, baby girl," she whispered.

Twisting around, I hugged her tightly. "Love you too, mom."

Letting me go, we went back to work, emotions high but with the knowledge that our family was survivors...and with the knowledge that James would have wanted us to survive.

The meal was soon ready and the table set for three, when there was a knock on my door. Glancing toward my parents, I shrugged before walking over to open it. Then I screamed as I stood in the doorway of my home, my mind not accepting what my eyes were seeing.

"Hi Alicia," Ben said, his smile beaming at me.

"OH, MY GOD!" I screamed again, as my body reacted instinctively and I immediately leaped toward him.

Ben's hands were full of flowers, but he dropped them just in time to catch me in his arms. I slammed into his chest and he picked me up easily. My heart pounded against his chest as his arms encircled me. He lifted his head and looked over my shoulder as I squeezed him tightly.

Ben saw an older couple standing inside the house

staring out at the commotion. Still carrying me, he stepped inside, out of the cold, and set me gently down on the floor while keeping his arms around me.

"Alicia," he said, as he peered down at my face, "are you okay?"

"How? How are you here?" I cried, my hands shaking.

Before answering, he stepped over to shake dad's hand. "Sir, I'm Benjamin Fowler. I was good friends with your son, James."

Dad grabbed Ben's hand, clasping it tightly and shaking it firmly. "Oh, son, welcome home. Welcome home. I'm George, and this is my lovely wife, Arlene, James' mom."

Ben reached his hand out to mom but she drew him into a hug, pulling him in close. She looked up and said, "Oh, Ben, we are so glad to meet you!"

He smiled at both of them before looking back to me, his gaze focusing on my still-shocked face. "I got out a few weeks early," he said with a shrug.

Closing the distance between us, I smiled up at him. "That much I figured out!"

Chuckling, he added, "For those of us who were scheduled to return in early January, the order came down that we were going to be allowed to travel before Christmas." He sent a nervous glance toward mom and dad, his voice hesitant. "I...um...well, I don't have any family and," looking down at my face, "I didn't want to waste any time meeting you. So, I just came straight here. I just dropped by but will be heading out so you can get back to your celebra—"

The three of us immediately interrupted him, protesting that he must stay, which he agreed to easily with a grin.

"Oh, I had some things for you," he said, looking around before realizing he left them outside. Hustling back to the door, he picked up the flowers he had dropped, handing them to mom. "I'm sorry, ma'am, but they ended up on the floor when Alicia opened the door."

Laughing, mom said, "You mean when my daughter screamed and jumped into your arms! And please, call me Arlene."

Bending again, he picked up a couple of plastic grocery sacks and stepped back inside. He'd brought a bottle of wine, as well as a six-pack of beer. Handing them to dad, he said, "I didn't know which you preferred, sir."

"It's George and," taking the alcohol from him, he said, "the wine will make the women happy and this beer will suit me just fine!"

Breathing a sigh of relief that he had chosen well, he spared a glance at me, finding me still staring at him, a smile etched on my face. Walking over, he touched my cheek with his finger. Leaning down, he whispered, "I brought you something also, but I'll give it to you later."

Mom hurried back into the kitchen and poured two glasses of wine and offered beer glasses to dad.

"Please take your coat off and have a seat. We were just ready to sit down," I said, suddenly unsure of what to say as I ushered him to a seat.

Soon the nervousness abated as we talked, shared, and laughed. Ben moaned as he ate, saying the taste of homemade cooking was better than he could have imagined. I piled more on his plate, telling him that he needed to make up for missing mom's Thanksgiving meal.

After lunch, Ben pulled out the pictures he brought with him that had James in them. Mom and dad exclaimed over the photographs and listened carefully as he explained where they were taken and what they were doing. They had questions and Ben answered thoroughly, understanding their need to hear of their fallen son.

I sat cross-legged on the floor, looking at the pictures scattered across the coffee table, my gaze constantly drifting over to my Christmas surprise. He was more handsome in person and I drank him in. Brown hair, still cut short. Wide shoulders and muscular chest, showcased in a light-weight, navy sweater. His jeans molded perfectly over his thick thighs. And right down to his cowboy boots, I took it all in.

Mom wiped a few tears along the way as dad's arm

stayed wrapped around his wife's shoulders, but they soon passed. After a few hours, they stood to take their leave. Hugging me, mom and dad whispered their love into my ear as they kissed me goodbye. Dad shook Ben's hand and invited him to their house as soon as he could come. Mom threw her arms around him again then had him bend down so she could kiss his cheek.

Chapter 11

(Ben)

THE DOOR CLOSED behind Arlene and George, and I turned back to Alicia, my stomach clenching with nerves. I stared at the beautiful woman in front of me, unable to take my eyes off her. Her long brown hair hung in waves down her back. She was a head shorter than me and when I had hugged her earlier, I noticed that her head tucked perfectly underneath my chin. Dressed in a holiday-red sweater and blue jeans, both showcasing her curves, my heart began to pound, realizing we were alone for the first time. My cock jumped at the thought, but I willed it to behave, not wanting to scare her off.

Trying to think of something to say, I just continued to stare until she grinned and I saw her slightly crooked smile. And that expression melted my unease.

Lifting my hand, I reached for her and she hurried to my side. Looking up, she said, "Will you stay for a while?"

"Nowhere else I'd rather be," I said honestly, allowing her to lead me to the sofa. This time, we sat next to each other, our legs touching. Reaching into my pocket, I pulled out a small, wrapped box. "This is for you," I said, handing it to her, smiling as I watched her wide-eyed surprise.

Alicia gasped before beaming, taking the gift. Unwrapping it quickly, she opened the lid of the box and revealed a pair of delicate silver earrings. "Oh, my goodness," she exclaimed. "They're exquisite!"

"I got them on base by a local Afghan who made them. I used to watch him work and, well until you, I never had a reason to shop. But as soon as they told me I was shipping back, I had him design these just for you."

Taking out her studs, she slipped the earrings into place and gave her head a little shake. Her smile dropped as she moaned, "But I didn't get you anything."

"But you did!" Seeing her puzzled look, I pulled out a piece of paper and showed it to her. "I've been going through the lists of possible mechanic's jobs in the area and have narrowed it down to some of these. I'll start interviewing in a few weeks once my discharge is complete."

Her eyes grew wide as my words hit her. "You're going to move here?"

Licking my lips nervously, I held her gaze, searching for an indication of her true feelings. *I hope I haven't read her wrong.* "Alicia," I began, taking her hands in mine, "you've become the most important person to me and even if we're just friends, I'd like to be near you as long as you're okay with that."

She jerked her hands out of mine, startling me until she threw them around my neck. "Yes, yes!" she cried. "I feel the same about you."

Settling on the sofa, now curled up together, we talked and shared for hours with Christmas music playing in the background. I couldn't imagine a better way to spend the day.

As the moon rose in the sky, I knew it was getting late and needed to leave, but hated the idea of not having her soft body tucked in close to me. Sighing, I said, "I need to go. I saw a hotel not too far from here. And then I thought I could take you to dinner tomorrow night." Standing, I held my hand out to her.

"What are you doing during the day tomorrow?" she asked, beaming up at me.

Shrugging, I replied, "Nothing."

"Then let's spend the day together. I owe you a trip to Walmart!" She stood too and held on to my hand as she nervously held my gaze. "And, you can stay here. I have a spare room. Um…it only has a twin bed but—"

"Are you sure?" I asked, my heart pounding once more.

Giggling, she nodded. "Yes, I'm sure. There's no

reason for you to spend money on a hotel when I've got a bed and separate bathroom here. And," she cocked her hip and joked, "I think I can trust you."

Stepping up so close that my boots were in front of her pink-painted toenails, I looked down and cupped her cheeks with my hands. "You can trust me with your life," I promised.

Looking up, she leaned toward me, but determined to be a gentleman, I bent forward and my lips touched her forehead. And she melted into my embrace.

That night, tucked into her guest room bed, the moonlight peeking through the slats in the blinds, I slept better than I had in years.

THE NEXT MORNING in Walmart, I grinned continuously even though I felt overwhelmed with the choices. I pushed the cart alongside Alicia, feeling domestically contented, as she pointed out everything she thought I might need. Afterward, she drove us to McDonald's where we indulged in Big Macs and fries, along with chocolate milkshakes.

Later, we drove to her parents' house and spent a few hours enjoying their company as well. George and I talked about mechanic garages.

"Son, my brother-in-law is a mechanic—taught

James all about cars from the time he could stand. He owns a large garage in Virginia Beach and he'd love to talk to you. Even if you don't work for him, he'd be a great person to help you figure out what to do."

Heaving a sigh of relief, I thanked George profusely and then watched as George called his brother and set up a time for us to talk. Looking over at Alicia, her smile warmed my heart.

That night, taking her out for our first date, I sat across from her at a little Italian restaurant. Sharing a corner booth, we sat with our legs touching and my arm over her shoulder as we waited for our food. No longer shy, we talked incessantly, and when the waitress brought our meal, we separated reluctantly.

"So, which do you like better? The Big Mac or this lasagna?" she asked, mozzarella cheese stringing from her mouth to her fork.

"God, it all tastes amazing," I admitted. "Everything just tastes better now."

"And Walmart?"

"Holy shit!" I exclaimed, my eyes wide. "That place was overwhelming after a year of not having any stores to shop in!"

Laughing, we finished our meal and ended the evening back on Alicia's sofa again. "Will you stay again?" she asked, her eyes hopeful.

Cupping her cheek, I replied, "Alicia, the past two

days have been the best of my life, but I don't want to take advantage of you. I never meant to come back and insert myself into your life so quickly." Seeing her furrowed brow, I rushed on, "I mean, it's a dream come true for me to be here with you. You and your parents...hell, even James, have shown me more about family than I've had in a very long time. And, you gotta know, I'd like to see where you and I can go." Feeling her relax in his arms encouraged him to continue. "But I need you to be sure and not feel rushed."

"I'm sure. I really want you to be here with me also," she confessed, her face looking up at mine.

I looked at her cupid's bow mouth and could not hold back any longer. Kissing her softly, my lips barely moved over hers until she moaned into my mouth. Unable to resist, I slipped my tongue into her warmth, reveling in the taste and feel of her. Learning her mouth, I pulled her close, feeling her curves pressing against mine.

Bending I picked her up and she wrapped her legs around my waist. Our lips never separated as I walked back toward her bedroom. Entering, I stopped at her bed. Leaning back to see her face, I said, "Tell me what you want, Alicia."

"You...I just want you," she replied, her eyes filled with lust as her kiss-swollen lips parted.

I let her body slide down my front, my erection

pressing against her stomach. My hand moved to the bottom of her sweater and I slipped it underneath the hem, skimming over her petal soft skin. She mirrored my motions by sliding her hands underneath my shirt, feeling the taut muscles of my back before moving them around to the defined ridges of my abs. Her hand brushed my erection and I gasped.

"Alicia, baby, it's been a really long time. There's no way this first time will last long, but I promise to take care of you first. But," I warned, "when I get inside, I won't be able to go slow…not the first time."

Licking her lips, she smiled up at me as she stripped her sweater up over her head, dropping it to the floor. My gaze fell to her breasts spilling out of her lacy bra.

"Fuckin' hell, you're gorgeous," I breathed, my finger trailing over her luscious mounds.

Her hands went to her jeans and as she shucked them down her legs, she teased, "You're overdressed."

When her jeans hit the floor, I pulled my sweater over my head and her breath came out in a whoosh as she gazed at my physique. My jeans were next and I jerked my boxers down at the same time, freeing my aching erection.

Deftly unhooking her bra, her rosy-tipped breasts were now exposed to my admiration. Bending, I scooped her up in my arms and deposited her gently on her bed. Standing over her, I knelt on the floor, reaching up to snag her panties in my hands. Pulling them slowly down her legs, I exposed her glistening folds to my view. The scent of her arousal hit me and I nearly wept with need. Determined to pleasure her first, I tossed her panties to the floor and moved her thighs apart with my broad shoulders.

Diving in, I latched onto her clit with my mouth, causing her hips to lift off the bed as she fisted the sheets. Like a feast to a starving man, I licked, sucked, and devoured her sex as my tongue ravaged her.

★

(Alicia)

LIFTING MY HEAD to peek at the handsome man between my legs, I moaned as my body coiled tighter. With one last nip on my clit, my orgasm flowed over me, the electricity from my core jolting out in all directions. His name wrenched from my lips, I threw my head back onto the mattress, my body slowly coming down from heaven.

Grabbing a condom from his wallet, Ben slid it on his engorged cock. Crawling over my body, he looked down at my relaxed face. "Baby, I'll try to take it slow—"

I stopped him by grabbing his head and pulling him down for a kiss. Tongues tangling, I moaned, "Not slow!"

Placing his cock at my entrance, he plunged deep inside, moaning, "You're so tight. Hang on, baby…I'm trying to make this last, but you feel so good." He began to thrust in and out, saying he wanted me to come again.

Wrapping my legs around his hips, I dug my heels into his tight ass, urging him on. My hands roamed from his shoulders down to his waist and back again. My sex began to tighten again and I gasped, "I'm close. So close."

As he reached between our bodies to press his thumb on my clit, I cried out his name once more as he threw his head back, his neck straining through his orgasm. Continuing to drive into me until he was drained, he fell to the side, his arms pulling me with him.

Legs tangled as our bodies slowly cooled, I could not remember ever feeling so content in my life. Looking down at me, Ben brushed my damp hair from my face, and I smiled up at him. "I'll be right back," he said, kissing me lightly. Watching him slip into the bathroom, I knew he took care of the condom before stalking back into the bedroom.

I leaned up, resting my head on my hand as I admired his naked body as he stalked back to me. Scooting over, I gave him room to slide in next to me.

Enveloping my body with his arms, he pulled me in, my breasts crushed against his chest, my head on his shoulder. As we began to explore each other bodies, he promised, "Now, I can go slow and savor every inch of you."

And, much to my pleasure, that's just what he did.

Chapter 12

(January – Alicia)

A MOUNTAIN CABIN in the snow…could it be more perfect? Rolling over in the early morning light, I smiled as I watched Ben sleeping. His face relaxed in slumber, I could not help but reach out to touch his muscular chest where the sheet had slid down. Waking, he smiled before opening his eyes, the feel of my fingers on his skin trailing heat wherever they touched.

I laughed as I threw my leg over his hips, bending down to kiss his lips. Soft and strong, I loved the feel of his mouth on mine. The kiss began slowly, but soon morphed into something wild.

Sitting up, I pulled the worn, soft, Army t-shirt I slept in over my head. He reached his hands up and cupped my breasts, palming their fullness as he tweaked my nipples. Throwing my head back in laughter, I thrust them further into his hands. Bending forward again, I reached over to the nightstand and grabbed a condom, ripping the package and rolling it on his impressive erection.

Lifting my hips, I positioned my awaiting entrance over his cock and with a swift move downward, impaled myself on him. Both of us groaning in delight, I began to rock back and forth, building the friction we craved.

(Ben)

I WATCHED HER face as she gazed down at me, her eyes shining brightly and her smile piercing my heart. With her hands on my shoulders, she worked my shaft until I knew I was ready to blow. Moving my hands from her nipples to between our bodies, I lightly pinched her clit and watched with satisfaction as she gripped my shoulders, moaning as her orgasm held her in its grasp.

Feeling her slick channel grab my cock, I took over, pistoning in and out until with one final thrust I pulsed through my orgasm. As she fell forward, I took her weight easily, my arms encircling her. As our bodies cooled and our heartbeats slowed, I slipped away to take care of the condom before rejoining her in bed. We both fell asleep again, bodies and hearts tangled together.

Awaking an hour later, I discovered the bed was empty. Swinging my legs over the side of the bed, I pulled on socks, sweatpants, and a t-shirt. Grabbing something from my suitcase, I padded out to the living room. Alicia was standing at the open front door of our rental log cabin, a steaming cup of coffee in her hands.

As I moved up behind her, I looked out the door to see the snowy vista of the Blue Ridge Mountains.

After weeks of out-processing with the Army, I took a job with Alicia's uncle, as a mechanic in his huge garage. But before getting started, I had one more thing to do on my list. We had been to the beach, eaten out, run in a park, and now, I wanted to spend my first snow, since being back in the States, in a cabin in the mountains.

Wrapping my arms around her from behind, I rested my chin on the top of her head and breathed in the cold, fresh air. Beautiful. Simply, fuckin' beautiful.

Alicia twisted in my arms, bending slightly to set her coffee cup on the table as we closed the door to keep the warm air inside.

Smiling down at her, I said, "I know Christmas is over, but I've got one more present to give you."

"You are spoiling me," she protested then, eyes wide, gasped as I dropped to one knee.

Looking up, I said, "I was so lost, Alicia, until James came into my life and became the brother I never had. I thought losing him was the end...but I know that it was only the beginning. Because you came into my life. And now I can't imagine life without you in it. Will you marry me?"

"Yes, yes," she cried, dropping to kneel with me, her arms encircling my neck. Her face just inches from mine, she said, "I never thought anything could come close to the bond I had with James and while our relationship is different...you are my other half. What we've shared over the last year has solidified our bond of love."

★

(Alicia and Ben)

TWO YEARS LATER, Alicia gave birth to a baby boy and Ben snuggled on the hospital bed with his wife and son in his arms. The door opened as Arlene and George entered.

"Where's my grandson?" George whispered, beaming with pride as he peeked at the sleeping baby in his daughter's arms.

"Oh, how precious," Arlene cooed. "Have you decided on a name?"

Alicia and Ben smiled at each other before facing her parents. "Mom, dad," she said, "meet James Benjamin Fowler."

If you enjoyed Bond of Love, please leave a review!

Letters From Home Series
Class of Love

Freedom of Love

Keep up with the latest news and never miss another release by Maryann Jordan. Sign up for her newsletter here!

goo.gl/forms/ydMTe0iz8L

Other books by Maryann Jordan
(all standalone books)

All of my books are stand-alone, each with their own HEA!! You can read them in any order!

Saints Protection & Investigation
(an elite group, assigned to the cases no one else wants...or can solve)

Serial Love

Healing Love

Revealing Love

Seeing Love

Honor Love

Sacrifice Love

Protecting Love

Remember Love

Discover Love

Surviving Love

Alvarez Security Series

(a group of former Special Forces brothers-in-arms now working to provide security in the southern city of Richland)

Gabe

Tony

Vinny

Jobe

Love's Series

(detectives solving crimes while protecting the women they love)

Love's Taming

Love's Tempting

Love's Trusting

The Fairfield Series

(small town detectives and the women they love)

Carol's Image

Laurie's Time

Emma's Home

Fireworks Over Fairfield

The Fairfield Series

(small town detectives and the women they love)

Carol's Image

Laurie's Time

Emma's Home

Fireworks Over Fairfield

Baytown Boys Series

Coming Home

Just One More Chance

Letters From Home Series

Class of Love

Freedom of Love

I love to hear from readers, so please email me!

Email

authormaryannjordan@gmail.com

Website

www.maryannjordanauthor.com

Facebook

facebook.com/authormaryannjordan

Twitter

@authorMAJordan

More About Maryann Jordan

As an Amazon Best Selling Author, I have always been an avid reader. I joke that I "cut my romance teeth" on the historical romance books from the 1970's. In 2013 I started a blog to showcase wonderful writers. In 2014, I finally gave in to the characters in my head pleading for their story to be told. Thus, Emma's Home was created.

My first novel, Emma's Home became an Amazon Best Seller in 3 categories within the first month of publishing. Its success was followed by the rest of the Fairfield Series and then led into the Love's Series. From there I have continued with the romantic suspense Alvarez Security Series and now the Saints Protection & Investigation Series, all bestsellers.

My books are filled with sweet romance and hot sex; mystery, suspense, real life characters and situations. My heroes are alphas, take charge men who love the strong, independent women they fall in love with.

I worked as a counselor in a high school and have been involved in education for the past 30 years. I recently retired and now can spend more time devoted to my writing.

I have been married to a wonderfully patient man for 34 years and have 2 adult very supportive daughters and 1 grandson.

When writing, my dog or one of my cats will usually be found in my lap!